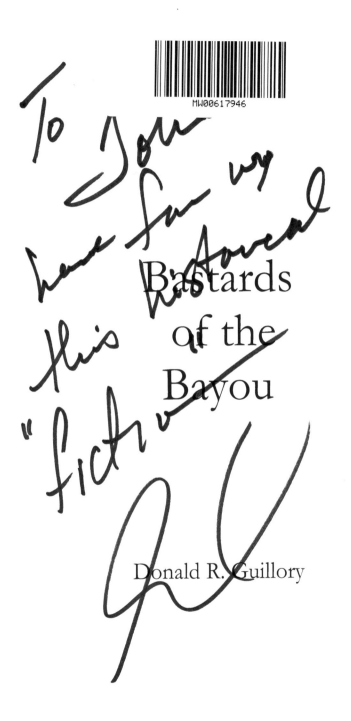

Bastards
of the
Bayou

Donald R. Guillory

ISBN: 9780997628111

DEDICATION

This book is dedicated to all those who wander the world aimlessly trying to figure things out while making it look like they have their shit together…

CONTENTS

ACKNOWLEDGMENTS

This book would not have been possible without the
support of my family, Havana Club Rum, questionable
internet searches, and reruns of "The Office."

Laveau

May 1978

The air was thick and humid as the sun set on Laveau. Located in St. Gerard Parish, just outside of New Orleans, it was home to the hard-working, hospitable, and God-fearing. The residents were a mix of skin colors, languages, nationalities and backgrounds. Everyone knew everyone. They knew each other's families and would band together in times of joy or in times of peril. It was a town where no one was ever left behind. Despite being in the deep south, the people did not segregate themselves as much as was experienced in other towns throughout the south. Unfortunately, that did not make them immune to the bigotry and hatred that had been woven into the American fabric.

The weekends in this sleepy town were typically the liveliest time for residents as it allowed them to unwind after a week of working on their farms or on the oil rigs. At the center of the town stood St. Richard's Catholic Church. It was an imposing structure that traced its founding to the French whom had settled and claimed the area as part of their quest to compete with Spain in the New World. The building had outlived generations of white, black, brown, and indigenous residents. It had survived head on collisions with the most powerful forces of nature and was a testament to the resilience of the community and region. It could not be brought down.

St. Richard's ensured the bonds of the community stayed intact even as some families moved away to find better opportunities in Texas, New York, Illinois, or California. The Church would come to serve as more than a place of worship. The weekends bore witness to an assortment of social events. People throughout the Parish would visit for a good meal and to socialize with relatives and friends. Often, someone would pull out an accordion and the townsfolk would begin dancing to Zydeco under the stars.

As years passed, the church became less of a focal point. For many of the youth, they began to see St. Richard's as a venue that offered them freedom from their homes. The words "I'm heading off to Saturday youth service" were not met with objection from the parents as they saw it as their children attempting to be closer to God. The clergy offered this time as a way to get to know the youth of Laveau and St. Gerard Parish so they could determine how best to serve the community's needs. Some parishioners showed up with genuine interest, while others used it as an excuse to get away from the prying eyes of their families and neighbors. They were free to meet with someone who caught their attention and commit acts that their parents would frown upon.

Teens would often meet up outside of the Church Hall which held its share of wedding receptions and birthday parties in order to get some alone time. As this gained in popularity, more and more of the younger residents would show up thus making it a less intimate affair. It eventually became so out of hand that the youth would have parties complete with music, food, and the occasional spirits to help liven up the affairs. It became a rite of passage for the youth of Laveau. It was something that made you complete. It made you part of the history of the town. The priests overlooked what took place as they understood the need for these kids to let loose. It also offered the priests the opportunity to get a head start on how they would counsel them when they would eventually visit the confessional. Most parties were uneventful other than a couple of young men fighting over a girl which often resulted in both parties going home alone. One night ended in anything but a peaceful resolution.

All the young men began their preparations for that weekend. They could be seen in town getting fresh haircuts or washing their cars. Some went so far as to buy a new shirt or cologne in order to have it serve as an icebreaker with the ladies. They were truly looking forward to meeting up with girls who were bold enough to sneak out of the house. They were all hoping that they would "get lucky" and find themselves in the amicable embrace in the backseat of their cars or behind the church. Despite all the effort that was put in, most gatherings resulted in most of the young men hardly getting past second base. This didn't dissuade them from lying about their sexual conquests throughout the week to their friends.

James Boone, oozed of wealth, privilege, and arrogance. The Boone family had been in St. Gerard Parish for generations and owed their wealth to the sugar plantations they had owned since before Louisiana was a state in the Union. James was the prototypical southern white teenager. He had no qualms about flaunting his family's wealth. He thought, rightfully so, that it would get him extra attention from the ladies and admiration from his peers, especially in St Gerard Parish. His charm had run thin with the young ladies at Louisiana State University, however. Coming home offered him the opportunity to pursue women without much effort. Many of them had never left the town of Laveau, let alone the Parish. Wherever James was, other people wanted to be there. He took care of his friends often by buying the alcohol for their get-togethers and even hiring a band to come and play at homecoming.

He arrived at St. Richard's as the usual crowd was gathering.

"What are we getting into tonight, fellas?" asked one of the men in the crowd.

"I think the real question is *who* are we getting into tonight?" He yelled over to a group of his friends as he approached them laughing and cocking his head back to further solidify his place with this assembly of bodies. James was the only one of them in college. He had just finished up his last year of law school while the rest were still working on their family farms or for the petrochemical companies nearby. The young men continued joking with one another as they enjoyed each other's company and beer despite no young ladies being within ear shot.

"So, y'all think the Tigers have a chance this year?" Brandon asked the group.

"A chance at what? They'll be lucky to beat Tulane next fall," James replied.

"All I care about is that they beat Ole Miss, ya hear?" Terry offered before spitting his tobacco juice on the ground.

The group continued talking sports and catching up as they waited for any girls to show up.

Father Charles, the Parish priest, stepped out of the church and approached the crowd of young men He was an intimidating man and imposing figure even without his collar and black suit. His eyes seemed to not just look at a person, but into them. He was the ultimate authority in that town. He held their secrets and was the gatekeeper for their salvation. It was understood that if you wanted to get to Heaven, you had to go through Father Charles.

"Good evening, boys. I trust you will all behave yourselves tonight."

They made poor attempts to hide their drinks behind themselves and out of the sight of Father Charles.

"Yes, father," they replied in unison.

He pulled a drag off his cigarette looking in James' direction. "Welcome back, Jimmy," he stated as he blew the smoke out through his nose. James hated being called that. His parents didn't go so far as to call him 'Jimmy' anymore. Once he hit his teen years, he wouldn't respond to anything other than James from his friends, folks, or teachers. It made him feel like a man. Jimmy made him feel like a little boy. Father Charles was the only one who would dare to call him that, and more importantly, he was the only one that James would not challenge for the infraction.

"Good to be back father. How have you been?" He asked nervously.

"I'm in the Lord's service so things are always well" he replied as he stamped out his cigarette with his foot. Looking back up to James, he gave a curious look. "Jimmy, it's been a while that you've been away. Have you been keeping up with your confessions?"

"Well..." He was hesitant to respond.

There was little thought that he gave to church or keeping up with traditions while away at school. The closest he had come to prayer was during finals week.

"So, I would be right in assuming that you're overdue?"

Before James had a chance to respond, Father Charles swooped onto him and took James under his arm. He patted James on the chest as he walked him toward the entrance of the church. As they passed through the vestibule, James noticed that the church was eerily quiet and empty. The only sign of life remaining was from the candles lit by parishioners earlier in the day.

"Father, this could wait until tomorrow. I just got back."

"No better time than the present, Jimmy. You know the routine." Father Charles gestured to the confessional. James reluctantly opened the door and knelt in front of the partition. Father Charles walked back to the doors of the church, locking them so they wouldn't be disturbed.

Father Charles returned to the confessional and knocked on the side of the wooden structure. James took this as his cue to begin.

He performed the sign of the cross which was more from muscle memory than from authenticity. "Forgive me father, for I have sinned. It's been…" he began before being interrupted by a faint voice in the darkness of the confessional booth.

"James?" a woman's voice asked from the other side of the divider.

He was taken aback.

Cordelia?

He hadn't heard her voice since he left for school the previous Fall. The soft soothing tone filled him with anxiety.

"Delia?" He whispered bewilderedly toward the mesh partition that divided the booth.

"It's me."

"How… How did you know I would be here?"

"I heard from my momma that you were coming back. Your parents love to talk about their golden boy."

"How's your momma?" James cautiously and anxiously asked.

"She's good."

"My folks wouldn't know how to get along without her. She's been with them since before I was born."

"I know. I had my share of days and sometimes, nights, without her in the house because she was taking care of your family's cooking and cleaning and raising you."

"How have you been?" James asked, nervously.

"If you're wondering about the baby, you don't need to worry. No one knows that it's yours."

"What did you tell your mother?"

"She never found out. I never really showed. She thought I was just getting big."

"I want to help, though. When I got your letter, I didn't know what to think. I'm sorry I never responded. I just didn't know what to do."

"I sent you the letter back in November. Anyway, it's nothing you need to worry about anymore."

"How's that?"

"I found someone to take care of it."

"Take care of it?"

Before the words could travel past her tongue, she was interrupted by shouting coming from the crowd that had gathered outside of the church.

"WHERE IS HE!?!?!?" an enraged young blonde shouted at the boys.

"Who?" Gerard asked.

He was no stranger to covering for James whenever a jealous girlfriend or jilted lover was looking for him. He played dumb as Candice Clark, James' current sweetheart, stormed toward him and his friends.

"*Who?* Who do you think? I'm looking for James." She shouted at the boys, poking her finger into their faces. "Y'all think I am damned fool. I know you boys come out here and get all liquored up hoping that you can stick your peckers in any little whore who's willing to drop her drawers for you."

"He was just here, Candice. He's over in the church with Father Charles confessing."

She turned her attention toward the church.

"James!!! JAMES!!! GET OUT HERE RIGHT NOW!!!"

He poked his head out of the confessional looking out the windows of the doors to see her silhouette before ducking his head back into the booth.

"Look. I'll be right back. Wait here and stay out of sight, Delia."

As he rose out of the confessional, Father Charles met him to unlock the door, letting him out to face the bedlam taking place under the trees outside of the church.

As James took three steps out of the church, he saw Candice. She stood no more than five feet, two inches tall, yet she seemed to tower over everyone assembled. Her short blonde hair bounced back and forth as she continued arguing with the boys whom she knew were stalling for James' benefit.

"Candice, what's with all the commotion?" he asked as he cautiously approached.

"Why are you out here? You come home from college and the first place you decide to go is here? You didn't come by. You didn't so much as call me. Do you realize how stupid that makes me look?"

"Look. I came out here to catch up with some of my friends. I was going to come by and see you."

"I know why you're here and it isn't about catching up with friends. I know that girl you used to sneak around with was coming here tonight. What are you doing? You going to run off with her?"

Cordelia was frozen as she hid in the confessional booth. She covered her mouth fearing that Candice might hear her outside. Cordelia placed her ear gingerly against the wall inside of the confessional. She could hear the entire conversation. Her anxiety grew as she heard footsteps and the laughter of the crowd come closer to the wall that shared the booth where she was seeking refuge. There was nowhere for her to go. There was nothing she could do that would allow her to escape without being seen or heard. If Father Charles had tried to usher her out, she could be seen which would confirm the suspicions that Candice had. It would make her predicament even more precarious. She was trapped.

"Candice, it's not like that."

"Not like that?" She crossed her arms aggressively. "Do you know how embarrassing it is knowing that the man your family has been pushing you to marry is out galivanting with some black trash? You think that going off to college would make you forget about her and focus on who you are supposed to be with. I promised to wait for you and marry you when you were done with school. I could have been running around entertaining offers from any number of the boys around here, but it was you I waited for."

A throng of people began walking over to the scene to watch the children of two of the more notable families of St Gerard Parish descend into chaos. They came over, drinks in hand and cigarettes dangling from their lips, as they began egging the situation on further.

"Just fucking kiss her. That'll shut her up!" Yelled out one of the boys.

Candice pulled out a pistol that she was

hiding in the small of her back, aiming the barrel squarely at James. Without knowing it, she pulled the trigger firing the gun in James' direction. It narrowly missed him, whizzing past his ear.

Ernest, who was trying to make his moves on one of the young ladies who showed up while James was in the church was startled as the bullet made its impact in the wall he was using as support. The bullet pierced the structure in between the space his fingers had left as he tried every pickup line he knew on the girl. He looked at the wall, glancing over at the cross through the window of the church and calmly and quietly walked back toward his car. He took it as a sign from God that this woman would not be right for him. He didn't say a word to anyone as he exited the scene.

"ARE YOU CRAZY?" James shouted as he fought the ringing in his ears.

"You are such a bastard. You can't even tell me that you love me."

Nervously, James exclaimed, "I love you, Candice. We'll get married. I promised you. Nothing changed."

"Then why are you here?"

"I told you, I'm here to catch up with some of my old friends. I might not get to see them too much this summer. Most of 'em are working in New Orleans or on the oil rigs. I just wanted to unwind and hang out with my friends before they left town. I wasn't sure of the next time I would get to see any of them."

Father Charles came running out of the church screaming, "Who the hell is shooting out here? Y'all are that drunk that you start whipping out pistols and shoot at a house of God?"

"It's okay, Father, just a lovers' quarrel," Gerard chuckled.

"Nothing is 'okay' with this." As he said that, he raised a bloody cloth. As James looked closer, he noticed that Father Charles' cassock looked wet. He touched it and pulled back red liquid on his fingertips.

"Father, are you okay? You're bleeding."

"It's not me you idiots! There's a dead girl in the church!"

James' face turned white. Cold beads of sweat trickled down his spine.

"Just get out of here Candice." James said

as he wrung his hands. "Gerard, take her home. We've got to figure something out."

"Sheriff's on his way," Father Charles informed the crowd. His voice deepened and seemed to echo in the darkness that had enveloped all of them. "Whatever y'all need to figure out, you need to figure it out soon. I'm going back in to pray for this poor girl's soul."

"Candice can't go to jail over this," Terry stated more out of concern than matter of fact.

"Why would she go to jail? It was an accident. We were all here and saw it," James replied. "We can't have her, or her family involved in this."

James turned to each of his friends and thought about how long they had all known each other. He thought about all the scrapes they had and the trouble they had gotten into together. These boys were like brothers to him and would follow him into hell and back if he had asked. "Look, Father Charles didn't see who fired the gun. Hell, he didn't even see the gun. Terry, do you still have your gun in your truck?"

"Yeah, but... no.... are you asking me what I think you are asking me?"

"We'll swear it was an accident. When the Sheriff asks, there are more people here willing to say that than won't if you take the fall."

"How are you going to ask me to do this?"

"Honestly, I can't say I would do the same if I were in your shoes. We'll get you a good lawyer and I am sure that I can talk to Candice's folks and mine to make sure you are taken care of. You'll still have your job at the plant when you get out and we'll take care of your family until you get back. If everyone out here swears it was an accident, the most you'll get is six months. I promise you. We'll take care of you Terry."

Terry nodded, convinced that this was the best solution for them all. He had had his run-ins with the law over the past few years and knew the routine quite well at this point. His only concern was how the new Sheriff would deal with him.

St. Gerard Parish had been under the jurisdiction of Sheriff Jeffrey "The Bulldog" Broussard since before these boys had been born. He held loyal to the concept of tradition which endeared him to the white population as he was seen as keeping the colored folks in line. The past year's election resulted in the Parish selecting a new Sheriff, Jean Papillon. He was only a few years older than James, Terry, and their friends. He campaigned on equality under the law and justice for all. It was not alarming on the surface, but for the affluent white constituents of St Gerard, their concern was that this meant an end to their "preferred status." Sheriff "Pap," as he preferred to be called, didn't concern himself with the color of his constituents nor how much money they had. The poor black and white folks saw him as a welcome change to their small corner of the world.

"I'm going to go and check on Father Charles. Y'all wait out here till the Sheriff shows," James said before walking back into the church. James looked over his shoulder to ensure that no one was following him or looking in his direction. His lips began to tremble as he crossed the threshold and saw a pool of blood coming out of the confessional booth. He slowly approached the structure where Father Charles was kneeling and praying. As he got closer, James saw that Father Charles was holding Cordelia's hand. She had died in that church, a place of refuge. She died violently and senselessly. James knew that if it had not been for him, she would still be alive, accident or not.

He wanted to see her. He wanted to push

open the door in the hopes that what Father Charles had said had been an error. She can't be dead. Not now. His fears were realized when he saw her limp body laying across the confessional bench. James' eyes widened as he saw her. Half of her face was missing. James knelt down in an attempt to comfort Cordelia's lifeless body. He was in disbelief at her being gone. Father Charles put his hand on James's shoulder. The touch unleashed a flood of emotions that he was feeling. He began to weep uncontrollably.

"Father, what do we do?"

"We pray, Jimmy. We pray."

They were silently reflecting and praying together when they heard the doors open behind them.

Sheriff Pap walked in slowly, trying to take in the scene.

"Father?"

"Oh yes, Sheriff. She's over here." He collected himself as he rose to greet Sheriff Pap.

The Sheriff walked over. James rose to give him space.

"So, what happened here?"

Before Father Charles could respond, James spoke up. "Well, we all got together outside to hang out and talk to the girls when Terry took out his gun to impress one of 'em. He forgot that it was loaded and accidently shot at the church."

Befuddled, Father Charles joined in on the story. "Yes, this young lady was in here confessing her sins to me when suddenly I heard a loud bang and cracking through the wall. Then I heard her fall to the ground."

"Father Charles came out and told that there was a dead girl in the church, so I came in here to help him."

"Poor girl. Either of you know who she is?"

Father Charles turned around grasping his rosary. "Her name is Cordelia LaFleur."

"Either of you know her?"

"Well, yeah. Her momma works for my family."

"Alright, well I'll notify the next of kin and call someone to pick up the body."

Sheriff Pap walked out of the church and

toward the crowd that had remained, minus a few of the girls who did not want their parents to find out that they were there, since the gun had been fired. He spoke to each of them and all of their stories matched up with what he was told by Father Charles and James. There was no need to investigate the matter further. He took Terry by his arm and sat him in the back of his car.

Father Charles and James stood in the doorway of the church as they watch Sheriff Pap drive away with Terry in custody. James let out a deep sigh as he placed his hands over his face. He knew that Terry had nothing to worry about. However, his worries turned back to the dead body of Cordelia. He wasn't sure if he was a father or not. Other than himself, Cordelia was the only person who knew about the baby. James had no idea where the child was, its name, if it was a little boy or girl. His only hope resided with Father Charles.

"Father, can I ask you something?"

"What is it Jimmy?" he asked, pulling out another cigarette.

"Did Cordelia talk to you about her ba-"

Father Charles held up his hand,

indicating for James to stop talking. It was the same tactic he had employed for years as their Sunday School teacher. When that hand was raised, your mouth would cease to be open. His ears were closed to any contributions that you thought were worthy of his time. Taking a deep drag from his cigarette, he looked through James.

"Go home, Jimmy," he said as he flicked the butt into the night air before walking back into the church.

Melancholy

Present Day

Michael sat in his office contemplating what purpose he had. He quietly reflected, counting the hours when he would walk out of his office. He'd been teaching at New Orleans University for roughly two years and had done little to advance his career. Even when holding office hours, he rarely ever saw students. This may have been due to his distant manner and his gruff demeanor. He hated living in the south and wasn't shy about it. He could often be overheard complaining about the heat, the humidity, and the relaxed approach to life that so many of the people there were accustomed to. They were foreign to him. Distant. There wasn't any link that he could see that he held to their existence. The truth is Michael was just bitter. This location and university were anything but his ideal choice in destination or work environment.

Michael continued sitting in his leather office chair as he heard the seconds tick away on the clock. He felt like a powerless monarch sitting on a throne that we wished he could abdicate. He looked up and saw that there were only forty minutes left in his posted hours. He despised office hours. They were pointless. Since his first day at New Orleans University, he had only one student drop by his office and that was when the young man was looking for another professor. It wasn't surprising.

History wasn't one of the sexier fields. Students in public school are taught to commit names, dates, places, and facts to rote memory with little consideration of the context or significance. What would these students want to discuss with him that couldn't be handled via email or over the phone? Students that did have a question or needed some sort of assistance ambushed him on the way to class or briefly after a lecture. This never changed despite reminders of his office hours. Perhaps it wasn't the lack of students that bothered him, but the abundance of time required by the university which he saw as excessive. Three hours each day regardless of one's teaching schedule was laid out by the faculty senate years ago. Perhaps this was their attempt to ensure that administration did not put exorbitant hours for instructors to have face to face time with their students. For Michael, this was overkill. It took away his freedom. He would rather pull up a stool at the bar and have a drink to end his day, but here he was waiting in what seemed like an endless dance where he was the only performer on the stage. The time had its benefits, though. Michael found himself reflecting on the path that brought him to this oversized chair in an office that overlooked a small pond and much of the campus.

He felt he was relegated to academic purgatory especially after teaching at Yale whose name alone meant that you were someone just by being associated with it. All he had to remind him of his time there was the degree on his wall, a stuffed bulldog, and the unfulfilled promises of tenure. Being in the Bayou allowed for him to get away from the debacle that plagued him during his last year in New Haven. It also afforded him the ability to get away from his ex-wife.

Before accepting the position with New Orleans University, he was absolutely miserable. The one thing that broke his melancholy was the day he walked into the courthouse to submit his divorce paperwork. When the clerk told him the filing cost, he filled out and signed the check with smiley faces and added "Freedom Papers" in the note section. He found so much joy in the dissolution of his marriage that Michael kept his divorce papers framed and on the wall of his apartment and a copy in his office desk that he would take out from time to time to bring a smile to his face. He enjoyed the simple pettiness of it all. He was able to get out of the marriage unscathed. There was no alimony, no child support to pay, and no property of his was lost. He chalked it up to a learning experience that he would always be mindful of. All that was behind him. There was a fifteen-hundred-mile buffer zone between them. That was one thing that gave him solace about being in the foreign, muggy south.

Despite being in the area for little over a year, Michael had done little to explore the city and neighboring areas other than an occasional visit to Bourbon Street for a quick drink before heading back to his apartment beyond the noise and the lights of the city. He found that spot to be fairly quiet even with it being close to New Orleans. It didn't have the level of crime that people complained about when they found themselves within the city limits. St Gerard Parish was home to gambling, refineries, fishing, and farming. It wasn't exactly the hotbed of academia or social life that he had experiences in the northeast.

The clock kept ticking away.

Michael continued the countdown in his head before looking up and seeing that there were only three minutes remaining before he would walk out of the door and head to his car. He often imagined the countdown to exit his office as if he were waiting in Times Square waiting for the ball to drop on New Year's. As he looked down at his briefcase there was a knock at the door.

"Professor Wilkins?" a female voice asked.

"Yes," he replied without looking. He thought to himself how absurd it was for someone to address him this way when his name was on the outside of his door. It plainly read *Michael Wilkins, PhD. Why was there a need to confirm that it was him? Who in their right mind would pretend to be him only to sit behind this desk?*

"Come on in." He casually motioned for her to take a seat. Michael looked at the clock and it seemed to be mocking him.

2:58

Only two minutes remained until his liberation would have been achieved and this student's entrance chained him back to his desk.

"I'm sorry to bother you." A young female

student with short curly brown hair poked her head past the threshold. She slowly shuffled her way to the gray chair across from Michael.

"Rebecca, correct?"

"Yes."

Michael internally congratulated himself for getting a student's name right. He notoriously gave his students playful nicknames in order to try and remember exactly who they are.

"What brings you in?"

"Well, I was worried about the final."

"What specifically?" Michael asked, thinking about how odd it was for a student to plan ahead this early for finals week when his students just had their midterms and returned just this week from their Fall break.

"I have an internship that starts at the end of the semester. I was wondering if I could take the exam early so I could get home and start working."

Michael let out a soft sigh.

"'I'm sorry for asking and I don't expect to be given any favors, but this is an opportunity that

I can't afford to miss out on. I have to get out of town before the last week of the semester if I am going to be able to hold on to it."

"I understand the feeling. I need to get out of town myself," Michael said as he looked up at the clock.

3:01

The clock was mocking him. He wanted to get out of that room as he felt every ounce of his being getting sucked into the walls as if he were to become a permanent fixture in his office that archaeologists would one day find among the ruins of the University.

"Look, I'll let you come in early and take the exam if you really need to."

Her eyes widened and she moved forward to nervously shake Michael's hand.

"Thank you so much. You have no idea how much this means to me. I've been working myself sick through school. I couldn't get all the financial aid that I had hoped to and between my classes and two jobs, I'm surprised that I haven't dropped dead." She kept talking.

What part of "you got what you want" is she

not picking up on? Michael hated discussing anything beyond its resolution. When something is done, for him, it is over. There is no need for further discussion, explanation, or chit-chat. He wanted her to simply say thank you and walk away but she sat there talking endlessly about her schedule, what professors she hated, how much she loved his class, and her summer plans. A break came when his phone rang. Michael picked up the receiver. Disingenuously, he apologized to his student for the interruption.

"Hello?"

"Mike… who's the piece of ass in your office?"

It was Dr. Roland Matthews. Roland had been at New Orleans University years before he earned tenure and now that he was senior faculty, he cared little about anything other than observing the young women who found their way on campus. He thought that since Michael was single that he must share the same interests in chasing women that were nearly half of his age or younger. Covering the receiver, Michael turned his attention back to his student.

"I'm sorry, Rebecca. I'll email you a schedule of dates and you can let me know what works."

"Thank you, again Dr. Wilkins." As she rose from her seat, she dropped several papers out of her messenger bag. Trying to recover them, she knocked several more items off of Michael's desk.

"Oh my God, I am so sorry."

Frustrated, Michael gave a reassuring thumbs up to Rebecca in order to let her know that she had nothing to worry about. She grabbed the pencils and random office supplies and put them back onto Michael's desk before backing out of the office, closing the door behind her.

"I'm back," he stated as he returned the receiver to his mouth.

"So, what's going on tonight?"

"Nothing other than grading and filling in the time I have on this planet with nonsensical, repetitious activities until I take my last breath… just like every other day."

"Why are you like this? What is with all of the nihilism?"

"You call it nihilism. I call it realism."

"Anyway. What are you up to? I need a

wingman and everyone else around here has one foot in the real world and one in the biblical. You are the only one I can tolerate who isn't into all of this holy rolling mumbo jumbo."

"Another time, perhaps. I am truly swamped. I'm several weeks behind on grading and don't want to have to be burdened with stacks of papers during finals week. I'd much rather prefer having as little as possible to do that week."

"We should hit the town this weekend. You don't want to miss out on all of these single mothers, career women, and bachelorette parties. These women are getting one of their rare moments away from home and are looking to make a mistake. I for one would be happy to be that mistake they go home regretting."

Michael humored him with an uncomfortable chuckle.

"Maybe next time."

"Come on. You need some release. When's the last time you got laid or at least got a blowjob?"

"Phew. It's been a while. But I can't imagine anything like this one woman I knew."

"Oh yeah? She local?"

"Nah."

"Humor me."

"She was really something else. She was able to suck out my will to live."

"Ok, Mike, enough about your ex. If you don't want to get into any trouble this weekend, it's your loss."

"Talk to you later."

Michael hung up the receiver and sat back behind his desk. He looked up at the clock and was slightly disturbed to see that it was now 3:12. He gathered his belongings and shoveled the stack of papers that had gone disturbed by Rebecca. It was only when he swung the shoulder strap over his head did he notice the corner of a white piece of paper peeking out from under his desk. It was completely out of place. Michael kept his office in an impeccable condition. Students and colleagues often remarked that it looked as though it was an exhibit. Other than Michael's presence, one would think that it was an Ikea showroom.

Michael knelt to pick up the piece of paper

only to discover that it wasn't trash. What he found was a small, seemingly insignificant business card. The front of the card featured a black and white image of an old Victorian style building with a sign that read "The Magnolia" above the entry. Michael placed the card into his pocket before walking out of his office and heading home.

Chez Wilkins

Michael drove home accompanied by the hissing of the radio as it tried to receive a signal. The thing hadn't worked since he tried to save money by installing it himself. He chalked it up to a learning experience that would afford him the opportunity to learn more about something that wasn't humanities related. The drive was shorter than usual and brought him home early to beat the setting sun. Michael hesitated to put the key in the door to his apartment. He didn't want to be home, but he didn't want to be away from his sanctuary from the campus. Before he could contemplate this dilemma further, he opened his door and passed through the threshold.

As he reached into his pocket to empty them of his wallet, he pulled out the business card that his student had dropped. He looked at it again and gave it more attention than when he first discovered it. He found the font and images particularly interesting. There was a picture of a Victorian style house in the background that seemed to cover the width of the card.

He flipped the card over which revealed more writing on the back: *The Magnolia: Pride of Laveau since 1972.* At the bottom of the card, it read

2 for 1 drinks on Thursday Nights! Michael found this odd considering most nightclubs and bars reserved Thursday night for "Ladies Night" in their attempt to lure men with the prospect of eligible women. He never had such luck. Michael looked at his watch and saw this it was only 5:30 and a little too early to hit a nightclub.

He sat down and opened his briefcase pulling out a short stack of papers that he had put off grading for the past two weeks. Most of the time, he delayed grading as he found himself getting irritated at the simple responses that his students gave to the writing prompts. He felt as though if they didn't invest the time in providing a strong analysis, he didn't have to invest his time in prioritizing his attention on their papers. This often resulted in emails from some students who were worried about their standing in his courses. For others, it didn't even raise concern. For Michael, he felt that those who were not worried about their grades resigned themselves to the reality of their failure and would often drop the course before the midterm cutoff. The registrar would often remark to him, in passing, that his course must be one of the harder ones on campus due to his high attrition rate. He would usually give a curt reply while relishing in the joy of having fewer papers to grade at the end of the term.

He put pen to paper and prepared for a night where he would make his students' offerings look like crime scenes. Michael took a sick pleasure in covering their pages with red ink. Tonight was different though. He rose from his desk and walked into his kitchen to retrieve a beer from the refrigerator. There was little inside that registered any presence of human life inside of that box. Even normal bachelors or divorcees had at least a block of cheese gathering mold. Michael had nothing. He wasn't disappointed by the revelation, he found it rather comforting. He stuck his head inside the refrigerator to receive the cool air on his face and on the back of his neck. It was a welcome feeling given the heat and humidity; however, his thirst was not quenched.

Michael closed the door and walked to the counter where he had left his keys. Within minutes he could head down to the corner store and get a twelve pack of light beer or if he were fortunate, Bacardi would be on special. His plans were quickly challenged as he saw the card for the Magnolia again. He picked it up, inspecting it again. He looked over at the stack of papers and back at the card in his hand.

"What the hell do I have to lose?" He said with a chuckle as he stuffed his wallet in his pocket and gave the middle finger to the papers as he walked out of the door.

The Magnolia

Driving to the address, Michael didn't know what to expect. He had been to a countless number of dive bars, each with their own character, their own mark on the world. He figured that they were all the same aside from the characters that he would find inside.

As he walked up, Michael took a measure of The Magnolia. The picture on the card didn't do it justice. It was immense. If it were not on land, Michael would have confused it with the river boats that would cruise back and forth on the Mississippi River. He held his breath as he walked toward the intimidating building that had time, surroundings, and circumstances change around it yet seemed to remain as pure as the day its paint had dried. Every inch on the outside oozed of history.

As his feet hit the steps leading to the door the creaking boards spoke to him. They wanted to tell him a story but were speaking a language he had yet to comprehend. With his hand on the rail, he felt the presence of generations of people who had walked up that same set of stairs approaching the entry. The edifice had him spellbound. Images of women and men of years past walked by him.

41

He could smell their perfumes. He could hear their accents. He felt the full weight and grasp of the southern humidity, but it did little to deter him. He needed to see the inside. He wanted to bear witness to this fantasy as it became reality.

The spell he was under was broken as a man was flung down from the stairs that led to the entryway by an immense black figure. The man was hurled out and onto the lawn of the property as if he were a stone being skipped across a still pond. The reject hit the ground with a thud before struggling to get back on to his feet. He dusted himself off before waving his hat at the man who had just ejected him.

"See you next time, Carl. Tell your mama and them I said hello," he laughed as he shuffled to his truck and drove off.

The incident had Michael nearly as awestruck as the building did upon his first arrival. The tall black figure seemed to fill the entire entry way. He loomed over Michael making him feel smaller with each second that passed. As he looked the figure over, Michael made the mistake of locking eyes with Carl and was met with a less than welcoming glare.

"Can I help you with something?" His

deep voice reverberated through Michael's chest.

Michael struggled to get the words fearing that he would meet the same fate as the good old boy who was turned into a lawn dart only moments before.

"I… uh. I just came by for a drink."

"Then what the hell are you doing standing here talking to me for?

Carl sensed the fear in Michael and only permitted him enough room to pass with as little comfort as possible.

"Welcome to the Magnolia."

A Friendly Stranger

The inside was even more exquisite than what was witnessed on the outside. Michael became intoxicated with the surroundings. He felt transplanted to the late 19th century. Everything that he had read about and researched in graduate school paled in comparison to what his eyes bore witness to at this moment. Michael walked over to the long mahogany bar. Hopefully their drinks would make as decent of an impression on him as the architecture had.

"What are you having?" a caramel-colored woman with long curly hair asked from behind the counter. She gave Michael a friendly smile as he tried to remember what kind of drink he wanted to embrace for the evening. Her face was welcoming and the first one belonging to a stranger that he didn't meet with contempt.

"I'm not sure," he muttered.

"I've never seen you around here before, otherwise I would suggest 'your usual.' Considering that you aren't a regular, I'm thinking that a 'usual' will not do as it is not a possibility. Beer?"

"No. I… uh… give me a whiskey, neat."

"My kind of man."

Michael dropped himself into the only open stool at the bar. The young lady poured the drink and placed it on the counter in front of him.

"Thank you."

"No worries. It's kind of my job."

Michael pulled out his wallet to pay her for the drink and was quickly rebuffed.

"You can put that away for now. You're obviously a first timer, so consider it a welcoming gift. Besides, it looked like you really needed that drink."

"I don't want to get you in any trouble. Please, I insist."

"It's really no trouble. This is my mama's place. I'll make up the cost for that one drink by watering down someone else's." She laughed. "What is it you do for a living? You don't strike me as one of the roughnecks. You are too clean, too well-mannered. Your hands, from looking at them, don't look as though they have ever seen manual labor. Your accent is all wrong, so I'm guessing you are not from around here, either."

"You have definitely got me in a box," Michael responded as he took a drink from his glass.

"I'm Vanessa, and you are?" she said extending her hand out to meet his. This was only time Michael could recall actually feeling welcome when someone offered the gesture. It was genuine.

"Michael."

"Pleasure to meet you."

"Pleasure to meet you, as well." Michael felt comfortable for the first time since arriving in Louisiana. On the outside, he often presented himself as someone comfortable in a number of situations not limited to the academic world, but it was all a mask that he put on to protect himself from people who may want to take him on as some type of project that they deemed in need of "fixing." If it wasn't the "Bible Thumpers" on campus, it was his someone suggesting therapy, transcendental meditation, or Bikram Yoga. With Vanessa, even in this short moment of meeting each other, he felt at ease.

"So, again, what is it that you do for a living?"

"Well, I'm a history professor at Nola U."

"No shit?"

"No shit."

Vanessa poured whiskey into another glass and took a drink.

"What brings you all the way out here?"

"Well, I found out my wife was cheating on me and I just had to get away."

"What? Today? Wow. I am so sorry about that."

Michael gave a confused look. "No, it was a couple of years ago."

"Oh, I meant what brought you all the way out here to the Magnolia. If you are teaching at Nola U, you have any number of bars, dives, and strip clubs that you could get a drink in back there."

Michael let out a nervous laugh and finished the rest of his drink.

"I needed that."

Vanessa let out a soft, comforting giggle. Michael missed the laugh of a woman. He missed the touch, not just in a sexual way, but in a comforting one. The feeling that someone knows how you feel, what you are thinking, and nothing needs to be said in order for it to be confirmed.

Michael and Vanessa continued their conversation, moving beyond the awkward moment that had derailed them.

"Anyway, what the hell is a roughneck?"

"Ah, well it's the boys that work out on the oil rigs. It's just a cute name that they gained a while back." She looked over Michael's shoulder and pointed at a group of gentlemen that were standing behind him. "If you want a better picture, they look a lot like those guys behind you."

Michael took a quick turn to look at the men who were grouped together enjoying their beers and having loud conversation. He didn't see anything special about them. There was nothing that made them stand out. Truthfully, they blended in quite well considering that they looked as though they were cut from a template as each was wearing significantly worn blue jeans, caps, and shirts with their respective company logos. Michael was the one who stood out. He was still in the same clothes he had been lecturing in earlier in the day. Michael scoffed at the group and returned to his conversation with Vanessa. Raising his glass, he felt the need to learn more about the young bartender.

One of the roughnecks approached the bar and came uncomfortably close to Michael. This was especially disturbing considering that there was more than enough space at the counter without having to impose on Michael's privacy.

"Hey sugar. Can I get a refill?" he asked while holding out an empty beer bottle over Michael's shoulder. Michael could feel the man's elbow digging into his collarbone and the discomfort had provoked a sense of irritability that he had not experienced since he was poked in the chest by one of the members of his high school lacrosse team. Michael was generally even-tempered and did not bother looking for trouble. He often calculated all possible scenarios and outcomes when faced with any measure of confrontation. When it came to "fight or flight," Michael was no stranger to walking away. The combination of the personal space violation and pressure building on his collarbone caused the anger to well up in Michael. It didn't help that each movement of the man increased the discomfort that he felt. He knew that a simple "please" would not suffice to get this man off him. Michael felt emasculated by this man who was towering over him. He was invisible. He was powerless. Michael didn't want to become a victim to this stranger's offense. He felt something swell up inside of him as a knot built up in his throat. His chest tightened and his pulse quickened.

"Get the fuck off of me," he growled through his teeth. Michael swatted the man's arm off of his shoulder.

"Fuck is wrong with you, pal?" the man asked, bewildered.

"Ever hear of personal space, you inbred shit?"

Michael heard the words. It sounded like his voice, but he was so uncertain of what took place that he thought someone must have impersonated him. He avoided confrontation. He purposely steered clear of it. Time slowed to where he gained a moment to examine the surroundings. He and the roughneck were standing nose to nose. He could feel the brim of the man's hat touching his forehead.

"Mike, Terry. Calm down. Here's your beer, now go on back to your boys," Vanessa implored as she tried to ease the situation. "Do I really need to get Carl over here?"

Terry took the beer from Vanessa and gave Michael an icy glare. Vanessa poured another drink for Michael to pacify him and prevent any further escalation on his part. It was an attempt made in vain as Michael was not willing to let it go.

"You ever cross paths with someone and later realize that should have just left them alone?" He uttered as Terry was turning around to return to his friends.

He gave a dull look and took a sip from his fresh beer. Michael, staring back at Terry, downed the rest of his drink. Filled with a shallow sense of confidence, and emboldened by the alcohol, he finished his statement, "I'm one of those people that you should probably leave alone." Michael's posture was a pure façade. The only fight he had ever found himself in was with his brother over the who got to sit in the front seat of the car as kids. After their squabbling, their fight was fruitless as their father beat them both and made them walk home from the park. His experience with any type of physical confrontation was limited to the Kung Fu movies that played Saturday nights on the local stations when he was growing up.

Terry sized Michael up. "Whatever you say then."

He walked off from Michael and resumed his game of pool.

Vanessa had a shocked look on her face. "You alright?"

"Yeah."

"You should probably take it easy on the drinks from here on out if you want to stay out of trouble. Those guys are a special breed."

"What breed is that?"

"Assholes."

Michael smiled and the two continued their conversation only to be interrupted by the occasional drink order.

Michael looked at his watch. *10:17.*

"I better go. Thanks again. This is the first night in a long time that I can honestly say that I enjoyed since moving out here."

"Glad to be of help. Be sure to come back again."

Michael rose from the stool and walked to the door. The realization that he had not completed his grading nor prepared his lecture for the next day's class did not faze him. He felt revived walking down the steps to return to his car. There was something about the last hour and a half that triggered a renewed sense of vigor and appreciation for life. He found himself singing a couple of songs that had played on the jukebox while he sat at the bar talking to Vanessa. As he placed his key in the door, his mood was broken.

"Hey shithead!"

The voice wasn't playful. It wasn't welcoming. It was the last voice that he wanted to hear at that moment.

A Shot in the Dark

The humidity offered a layer of protection to Michael's ego that was sorely needed as he could attribute his profuse sweating to the climate.

Michael looked the men over. They were much larger than they appeared under the lights inside the Magnolia. Their faces were rough and unfriendly. Nothing about them offered an indication that they would buy Michael's bluff. They were no strangers to altercations. One had a deep scar on the right side of his head which was more pronounced with the short haircut he sported. Another was almost as wide as he was tall. His arms and hands made him look as though he pulled trees out of the ground at the root for fun. Their eyes were all fixed on Michael. He felt their gaze penetrate him. Their physical presence surrounded Michael while their odor consumed him. He was uneasy about the impending assault, but was more disturbed by the mixture of sweat, bourbon, tobacco, and petroleum that hovered in the air around these men, an aroma that swallowed up Michael.

There was nowhere for him to escape. There was no way of saving face. They were all focused on ending Michael's night.

"We gonna do this?" Michael was bewildered as he heard the words come out of his mouth. He hadn't so much as thrown his fists out to cheer during a football game and here he was facing down these three men that looked as though they emerged from the womb swinging.

Michael took a deep breath in, closing his eyes. He opened them narrowly, permitting him to focus on the one man directly in front of him. As he stepped forward, he heard a crash and felt an intense pain on the back of his head. His vision became blurry. His legs began to give way. He sank to the ground. The sharp gravel penetrated his arms, face, and chest. He struggled to get to his feet. It was pointless. Gravity continued to pull him back down. The crunching of the gravel and grinding of approaching footsteps filled him with anxiety.

He couldn't move. He couldn't speak. He felt someone hovering over him. Michael could only make out the silhouette of hands as he was blinded by the floodlights shining from the Magnolia. The hands moved at a tremendously slow pace. Michael could hear his heartbeat. He felt the pumping of his heart lifting him up and resting him back to the ground with each beat. He heard voices but could not make out any of the words being said. His eyes slowly closed as the hands grabbed him, lifting him to his knees.

The last thing he heard was the sound of a gunshot before his body dropped back to the ground.

Bastards of the Bayou

Wakeup Call

Michael's head was throbbing. He tried to rub the spot that ached, but as soon as he touched the it, he was struck by a sharp pain. As he opened his eyes, all he could see was blue. He blinked his eyes several times to clear his vision, wiping them as he opened them wider. The pain was discomforting and disorienting. There was ringing in his ears. He rolled to his side and looked at his surroundings. He was in a lavish room with blue curtains. There were black and white pictures in frames on the walls. The images behind the glass had yellowed over the years. Questions continued to circle his mind.

Where am I?

What happened last night?

As he moved to stand up, he felt nothing but the hardwood floors on his bare feet. They were surprisingly cold. Michael could feel every groove and imperfection as they contacted the soles of his feet. He sat up with his back to the wall. Holding his head, he tried to comprehend what actions brought him to this cold, lonely, room. As he sat there, he heard footsteps. They sounded like a giant was walking toward his room. It felt as though the steps were shaking the walls. The sound was making the Michael's headache even more. With each step, the old photos on the walls shifted and the water in the glass on the nightstand to ripple.

There was a gentle knock at the door.

"Good morning, Bruce Lee," a motherly voice chuckled from the other side of the door.

What is going on here?

The knob turned. The door opened and revealed a short, older, red-headed white woman in a flowing robe. The sleeves were long enough to hide her hands. As she walked toward Michael, it looked as though she was floating. She passed by the window and as the sun shone through it, she looked like an angel.

"How did you sleep?" she asked in her soft and raspy voice.

"Like Jesus during slavery."

"Pardon?"

"Sorry. This is the first time in a long while that I have slept through the night."

"Through the night? It's nearly noon. Well,

maybe you should spend more time in old brothels."

"I don't plan on making this a habit. Did you say brothel? I didn't know brothels were still around."

Michael's mind raced.

Had he spent the night with this old prostitute? He looked for his wallet to pay the woman.

Noticing his confusion, the woman comforted Michael. "Everything is fine. What happened last night was my pleasure. I was happy to do it for you. It made me feel young again. I haven't had blood flowing through my veins like that since I was, Hell, I can't recall, but it made me feel alive."

A cold sweat ran down Michael's back. He hadn't felt that uncomfortable since he was persuaded into attending a joint Bachelor-Bachelorette party for a friend of his.

"Listen, I, uh. I am sure that I owe you. I just don't know how much."

"A simple thank you would suffice."

"Just a thank you? I meant money. How

much?"

"Money?" the woman's face contorted to match her confusion.

A booming voice interrupted their conversation.

"Eleanor, you up here, gal?" a booming voice asked from the other side of the door.

"Come on up, Pap!" she called out to him.

"Are you decent?"

"Would I tell you to come in otherwise?" she laughed at the absurdity of his concern.

"Eleanor, that's exactly what you said last time and I walked in on you just as God made you."

"Consider yourself lucky. There was a time where seeing me like that would have cost you a pretty penny and possibly your marriage."

Michael whispered to Eleanor, "Pap?"

"Yes, Sheriff Pap."

His footsteps were coming closer.

Michael held his breath as he grew more

anxious. He tried to remember the events of the previous night. He thought about being in the room with Eleanor. He thought about the university hearing about what had taken place. He saw his face plastered across newspapers and on TV. *University Professor Arrested at Local Brothel!* He felt shame, the kind of shame that had met him on too many mornings the night after binge drinking in college. Instead of waking up in a strange dorm room lying next to some random undergrad, he found himself in the room of an old prostitute, naked. His only protection came in the form of Egyptian cotton sheets.

A faint knock sounded on the door. Eleanor rose with her extravagant purple robe flowing, making her look like a deity.

"Come on in," she sang as she stepped toward the door.

"Ok, I'm going to ask again. Are you decent?"

"Dammit, Pap. Right now, at this very moment, I can assure you that I am!"

The door swung open.

"And now I'm not!" Eleanor laughed as

her robe fell to the floor.

"Goddammit, Eleanor! I should arrest you for that shit!"

"Arrest me for what? Because you fall for it each and every time? Anyway, you like what you see too much in order to punish me for it," she said as she adorned her robe once again.

Eleanor walked up to Pap, taking his hat off his head and putting it atop her own.

"I'm the law 'round here," she stated in a gruff voice, mocking the Sherriff.

Pap was dumbfounded. He stood just over six feet tall, but his presence was even larger. His dark skin was magnified by the gray hair atop his head.

"Enough. Is this the troublemaker?" He asked pointing at Michael.

Troublemaker? What the fuck did I do?

"How you feeling, son?" Pap asked. His tone was more inquisitive than out of general concern. Michael felt it was closer to Pap trying to determine how much paperwork their interaction would require.

"I guess I'm ok. Other than this headache, I don't have any complaints."

Pap inspected the back of Michael's head letting out a whistle.

"Well, according to some of the calls I got last night, you took it upon yourself to fight an entire band of roughnecks."

"I vaguely remember arguing with a couple of guys, but other than that, I'm all foggy."

"So… you don't recall Ms. Eleanor saving your ass?"

The words entered Michael's mind and his brain was flooded with images of Eleanor attacking the group of men in a way that would rival Wonder Woman.

"I can tell from the confused look on your face that none of this registers with you."

Michael shook his head, partially denying any memory of the preceding night's events and partially to remove the idea of this gentle-looking woman engaging in physical combat.

"Eleanor, would you have your girl make us some coffee?"

"Sure enough, Pap." She buzzed the intercom and told the person on the other end to get a fresh pot ready.

"As for you, put some clothes on and come downstairs. We need to talk some more about last night."

Café au Lait

Michael struggled to his feet. The pain from his injury mixed with the fatigue and alcohol still coursing through his system rendered him even more sluggish than usual. The smell of the coffee coming from downstairs helped move his pulse a few beats higher. He grew to depend on those magic beans to get him through countless late nights and early mornings in graduate school. The sound of percolation was stronger than any alarm clock he had used over the years. He put one leg into his pants. Another whiff of the rich aroma enticed him. Michael's nose widened and the warmth filled his body. The second leg was now in. He caught a glimpse of himself in the reflection of one of the picture frames. He was almost presentable. His eyes were sunken. His hair disheveled. He turned his head in a vain attempt to preen himself for the inquisition that awaited him downstairs.

Michael pulled his shirt over his head and allowed it to fall, draping his body. He could hear the clink of spoons and ceramic mugs. He envisioned the swirling of the coffee, cream, and sugar.

The procession down the stairs made

Michael feel as though he were walking himself to the gallows of his own execution. Despite the reassurance that he was not in handcuffs, the guilt and self-doubt crept in and compelled him to condemn himself. As he reached the last step, he looked up to see Pap sitting at a table, drinking a freshly poured cup of coffee. Pap lifted his foot, pushing the chair opposite him from under the table.

"Have a seat."

Michael's throat tightened.

Pap could sense the tension and fed off of it.

"Look son, this is normally where I would fuck with you a bit and drag this all out, but I have a lot of work today. Besides, messing with you wouldn't be worth the reward for the work required."

Michael's shoulders relaxed as he felt his execution had been commuted.

"So, I just need a statement from you as a formality."

"But I thought Eleanor explained what happened."

"That's Ms. Eleanor to you. You don't know her well enough despite sleeping in her home last night."

Pap took out his ballpoint pen and clicked the end as he prepared to listen to what Michael had to say.

"Alright, whenever you are ready."

Michael's anxiety returned as the temperature of the room rose. He saw Pap's lips moving, but there was nothing audible. Michael nodded, not understanding anything that was being said. He had been through this before on a number of dates and candidate interviews when he was job searching. *What the other person had to say or ask wasn't nearly as important as what you had to say. They needed to hear certain things to believe you, to feel comfortable with you.* He recalled the advice that he had been given by his college career planner. Michael always thought that the advice was bullshit, until he put it into action. He opened his mouth and allowed the events of the night to pour out. Pap nodded, laughed, sipped his coffee, and kept writing.

"And that's when I woke up in the room with Eleanor, Ms. Eleanor attending to me."

"Ok. Anything else?"

"I can't think of anything. It truly was all just a blur. My mind is foggy on many of the details."

Pap finished his coffee and stood up.

"Come on outside with me."

Oh Shit! This is where it ends. This is where the freedom of Michael Wilkins. He had no next of kin to contact anywhere near the area. There was no one from the University that he could readily call for support without making his arrest into something more than it was. No one would be discrete about it. Michael turned from his anxiety about his possible arrest to how it might improve his standing. Students would be afraid to ask him questions knowing that he had a record. His Dean would be reluctant to ask him to serve on any extra committees. He played the scenarios over and over in his head thinking about how much he would be able to get away with now that he was labeled a menace to society.

Pap adjusted his shirt into his pants ensuring that he looked every bit a man of the law before handing the mug back over to Vanessa who was taking inventory and doing light cleaning at the bar.

"Tell your mama I said thanks. I'll come by soon."

"Sure thing, Pap. Thanks," she said with a warm smile.

"Thank you for everything, Vanessa," Michael said in a nervous tone.

"Of course, che. I hope to see you again."

Michael nodded as he followed Pap out of the front door. Regardless what his fate was, he wanted to see Vanessa again. The smile she gave as he exited reassured him, easing any anxiety about being alone with Pap.

Eye of the Storm

Pap led Michael down the stairs of the Magnolia. Michael was afraid to ask about the status of his freedom. Considering that he was not wearing a set of chrome bracelets, he did not want to risk his question dooming him. His concern over his security ended when Pap walked him through the parking lot.

Michael looked at his car. It was nearly unrecognizable. If it hadn't been for his vanity plate that read "DRDUBS." The tires had been slashed. The windshield had a rock thrown through it. Pieces of glass lay on the hood and the interior, sparkling in the sunlight. Someone had destroyed his car and he had a good idea of who it was. Michael looked it over and began to calculate every dollar of damage that had been inflicted. He also reflected on every penny he had put into the car over the years. Every mile on the odometer passed in his mind. He could still smell the roadkill that he had passed on his journey from New England to Louisiana which was especially pungent on the heavily humid Summer days. He wasn't angry at the sight of the vehicle in this state. Pap found Michael's silence odd.

"You seem a little too calm."

"Yeah. What can I do? Getting pissed off about it won't magically transform my car back to its former glory."

"Hmm. You sure it doesn't have anything to do with your recreational activities?" Pap asked as he made a smoking motion by pinching his thumb and index finger against his lips.

"What?" Michael was confused.

"Your plate. Come on son. Dr. Doobies? You'd have to be a real friend of Mary Jane to get a personalized plate like that."

Michael let out a short chuckle and resisted the urge to be a complete smartass with the man who now controlled his fate.

"No. No. No. That's Dr. Dubs as in 'W.' It's my initial. My students started calling me that years ago and when I had the opportunity to get personalized plates, I couldn't think of anything else."

"Yeah. That makes more sense. You didn't strike me as a pothead, but you never know."

Before Sheriff Pap could fully make amends for his poor situational assessment, his attention was diverted to a cloud of dust proceeding towards where they stood. A small luxury car was barreling down the gravel road. The car made its way into the parking lot and came to an abrupt stop. The dust continued in its direction toward Pap and Michael. A light film covered the surface of the Sheriff's glasses. Michael was stifled by the particles in the air. As Michael covered his mouth to fight off a cough, Pap pulled a small white handkerchief out of his pocket and cleaned his glasses.

The urgency of the vehicle was only matched by the individual who exited. A tall, lean, older white man opened the door and ran toward Pap and Michael.

"Sheriff, I heard about what happened last night. Whatever my boys did out here, I'll pay the damages."

"Small towns," Sheriff Pap chuckled as he returned the handkerchief to his pocket. "I swear, no one can take a shit without everyone knowing what they had to eat."

The man held out his hand awaiting Michael's in return.

"James Boone."

"Michael Wilkins."

"Pleasure to meet you. I wish it were due to better circumstances."

James inspected the car and his face filled with disgust in response to each bit of damage he saw.

"What exactly happened out here last night?"

"I thought you said you heard?" Pap replied.

"I only heard the basics that my boys got into a fight out here. I tried to call your office, but the line was busy. I was expecting to have to bail them out again."

"Yeah, I am going to have to have a talk with your nephews."

"Cousins," James corrected him. He looked at Michael. "They are my cousin's kids. They have always thought of me as their uncle due to the age difference and how close we are. Considering I don't have any boys of my own, I have always taken care of them when they needed something."

Sheriff Pap interjected, preventing Boone from delving deeper into a genealogical examination.

"Well, your boys and some of their co-workers got into it with this gentleman. Eleanor broke things up before it got really out of hand. I guess they weren't happy about her intervening and took it out on his car."

Michael, having come out on the worse end of the altercation, fought the urge to roll his eyes at the absurdity of the Sheriff's claim. *Did he have to be beaten within an inch of his life for things to "get out of hand."*

"Young man, I want to extend my sincere apologies. Their actions do not represent me nor this town."

Michael nodded more out of acknowledgement than agreement.

"I'll call you a tow truck," he said before pulling out his cell phone. He started punching the numbers in and held the phone to his ear as he awaited a response on the other end. "Whatever this costs, I'll take it out of those boys' pay."

Michael wasn't relieved at who would be

paying. His concern was focused on how he was further inconvenienced by not being able to just leave and put the previous night behind him. He was good at escaping from situations that made him uncomfortable. This was not an option for him.

James pulled the phone away from his ear and looked at the screen in frustration. Zero bars.

"Well, it would be a lot easier to make a call if I had a signal out here."

"You must never come this way then, Mr. Boone. The Magnolia is in a dead zone. Cell coverage is spotty, at best, but they have a landline inside." Pap offered. "If you'll excuse me, I need to take Dr. Wilkins to my office and keep him out of trouble.

As they entered Pap's truck, Michael watched as James Boone walked up the stairs of the Magnolia and through the doorway.

Past Tense

In all of his years living in Laveau, James Boone had never passed through the doors of the Magnolia. Today had been the first time that he had been on its grounds. With each step, James was less at ease. He ignored the bottles and trash on the veranda before stepping through the entrance. Inside, no one greeted him. He could not see anyone present. The only notification that he was not alone in the building was the sound of a swishing broom. He moved in the direction of the rhythmic sound and saw a young woman cleaning behind the bar with her back to him.

"Ma'am," he called out.

She continued along with her task.

James moved closer.

"Ma'am."

Again, he was unsuccessful at gaining her attention.

Frustrated, he tapped her on the shoulder gingerly. Vanessa pulled an earbud out without looking up.

"Yes, mama?" she returned as her head

raised, expecting to see Eleanor's reflection in the mirror behind the bar.

Vanessa, startled, stood straight up and swung around.

"Sir, we are not open at the moment, but please feel free to come back this evening."

"Sorry, honey. I didn't mean to startle you May I use the phone? Sheriff Pap suggested I come in here and use yours."

Catching her breath, Vanessa placed a push button cordless phone on the counter.

"Here you go. Let me know if you need anything else."

She put her earbud back in and continued cleaning.

"Thank you," James said as he punched the numbers into the phone.

"Ray's autobody" a gruff voice answered.

"Ray, this is James Boone."

"Afternoon, sir. What can I do for you?"

"Well, my boys got into it with a young

man over at the Magnolia last night and did a number on his car. I want to get it repaired and need you to come pick it up. I'm hoping that getting the car fixed will keep these boys from spending a night in jail. Would you be able to come over and tow it to your shop and get him squared away? You can send me the bill."

"Sure thing. It's still over at the Magnolia?"

As Vanessa continued cleaning the bar and arranging the bottles on the shelves, James watched as she worked. He wasn't acquainted with her, but she seemed all too familiar to him. As he gave Ray information about the visible damage and description of the vehicle, Vanessa faced him as she continued wiping down the area.

To avoid having Vanessa catch him looking at her, he looked off into the mirror behind the bar, catching his worn face in the reflection. The image looked back at him, mocking the years that had passed all too quickly reminding him that there was no stopping or reversing them.

James hung up the phone and motioned to Vanessa indicating that he was done. She removed the earbud from her right ear, sweeping the hair on that side behind her shoulder. As she reached out for the phone, James saw a small heart-shaped birthmark on her shoulder.

"Delia?"

"Pardon?"

"Oh, nothing. I was just thinking out loud. Thank you for letting me use your phone. You have a good day."

"You are more than welcome, Mr.?"

"Boone, James Boone."

"Vanessa. Come back anytime." She said as returned to her music and cleaning.

Eleanor stepped out of the shower. As she wrapped a towel around her body and another around her head, she heard his voice. She heard it clearly upstairs but had her doubts. Then he said his name.

James Fucking Boone

Eleanor clenched her teeth and wrapped her robe around her body. She walked down the stairs to see Vanessa standing at the bar, alone.

Vanessa saw the concern in her mother's face.

"Mama, you ok?"

"Was someone just here?"

"Yeah. A Mr. Boone."

"James Boone?"

"Yup," she replied as she dumped the contents of a dustpan into the trash can.

"What did he want?"

"Just wanted to use the phone. He said that he needed to call a tow truck for Michael's car."

"Yeah," Eleanor said, sucking her teeth.

Eleanor walked to the entrance and glared off into the distance hoping to catch a glimpse of James.

Houseguest

Pap and Michael traveled to the Sheriff's office passing over every manner of road and path. Pap made a few stops checking in on several residents. The stops ranged from general welfare to giving a ride to the grocery store for Ms. Buteau, a 98-year-old woman who insisted on living independently. Michael was amazed at the ease of pace that these people lived.

Pap pulled in front of an unassuming building at the town square and indicated to Michael that they had arrived at their final destination. Michael followed behind the Sheriff as they entered the office. The interior was just as unassuming as it was on the outside. There were a couple of plants that needed water due to the browning of the leaves. The pictures that hung on the wall featuring the pictures of former Sheriffs and news articles had not been dusted in some time. A small white-haired old woman sat behind a desk with her head down and the phone receiver to her ear. Sheriff Pap cleared his throat in a vain attempt to announce his entry. There was no response from the gentle creature seated before him. His second attempt had the same result. He lowered himself to within inches of her face.

"Alice," he sang to her. He stretched out her name and added extra syllables to it in order to keep the sound audible. "Wake up, Alice."

She struggled from her slumber, wiping the saliva from the corner of her mouth.

"Sheriff's Office, please hold," she stated as she placed the receiver against Pap's nose. The "off-hook" tone played faintly. There was no telling how long she had the receiver away from the base.

"Alice," Pap blurted out startling the old woman. Michael felt a bit uncomfortable seeing Pap yell at her, but part of him was glad that this moment of her suspended animation was over, reassuring him that he wasn't going to have to deal with a dead body on top of everything else that had occurred that day.

She adjusted her glasses, leaning back in her chair.

"Good morning, Pap."

"Alice, it is damned near five in the afternoon."

"What day is it?"

"Friday."

"You sure?"

"Yep. All day. Anyway. Did the mail run yet?"

Michael continued looking Alice over. She was the very picture that Hallmark and marketing companies would use to define what a grandmother was. Despite the heat, she was wearing a shawl over her shoulders. Her skin looked paper thin. She had left cookies out on the counter for anyone who may have come by needing a snack. Her desk was littered with papers, some with scribbles, some were typed out forms. And then he saw it. The little woman had a bowl of hard candy sitting out. Michael questioned the age of the candy. It looked to be a mixture of candies that would be appropriate for any holiday, occasion, or to allow one to fight off low blood sugar. An almost primeval, instinctive impulse hit him, urging him to grab at least one of the candies. He couldn't bring himself to pull off the feat out of the fear that he would come away with more than piece. His urge was completely stymied as he watched Alice lick her fingers before placing her hand into the bowl retracting a piece to satisfy her own need.

"Oh yeah. I put it on your desk about an hour ago. It's just the Church bulletin and some junk mail," she said as she sucked on a peppermint.

"Thank you much. Oh, and could you put a fresh pot on."

"Sure thing, Pap."

Alice picked up the receiver and dialed the numbers that she had scrawled onto the note as Michael followed Pap into his office.

"Have a seat" Pap said as he motioned toward the seat across from his desk. Michael thought to himself how this must feel for the few students that come to meet him in his office. His concern for his car and work was his focus. Pap unfolded the St Richard's Report, the bulletin for the local Catholic church.

"You a religious man, Sheriff?"

From behind the paper, there was a short "Nope" in response. The conversation was dead. Michael didn't know where to go in order to ease the tension and anxiety that he felt being with Pap. Topics circulated through his head; sports, politics, weather. Everything he thought couldn't possibly go that far with this man. There were no signs of sports allegiance in the office. There was nothing in the building that assigned him to any political affiliation other than the law. Nothing from the local Democratic or Republican party. The election poster featuring his name and likeness that was on the wall said nothing more than "Re-Elect Pap." Each thought was a dead-end. Michael thought that he was good at reading people, but Sheriff Pap seemed to speak a language that he was unaccustomed to.

"So. Anything interesting in the paper?"

"Not really. It is just the general events, marriage announcements, bingo schedule, church sports league schedule, complaints, classified sales, obituary, that sort of thing. All in all, it's pretty much the same every week. They send it out on Friday almost as a reminder to everyone about what events are taking place, what they missed out on. The one thing that you can count on being different each week is the obituary. The same person can't die with each publication." Pap continued reading and then came across something that caught his interest in the text. He abruptly rose and walked out of the threshold of his office and over to Alice's desk.

"Alice, you remember that Priest who used to work in this Parish? The one who the Church removed because he was a little too close to the prostitutes?"

"I don't recall."

"Come on. You know the one." In a hushed tone he insisted. "The one who got Eleanor pregnant and got relocated by the Church." Despite Pap's efforts, Michael could hear the conversation being conducted.

"Oh yeah. It was um… Christopher… No… Carl something."

"Charles?"

"Oh yeah. That was it. He was a pretty good priest. There wasn't a soul in town that didn't respect him. It was a shame that he got in all that trouble. Why do you ask?"

Pap placed the bulletin on her desk with the obituary page facing up. Alice picked up the paper and began to read the text of the message.

"St Richard's is saddened to announce the passing of Father Charles Stevenson at the age of 75. Father Charles served in 6 different parishes during his nearly 50 years as a priest. His parishioners remember him for his gentle presence, sound advice, and service that extended beyond the altar and into their homes. He was 'a part of all of our families' according to Melinda Stelly, the coordinator of the liturgy for St. Richard's where Father Charles was pastor for nearly 20 years."

Alice pulled her glasses from her face and allowed them to hang from the chain she had around her neck. She grabbed a handful of tissues from the box on her desk to wipe her eyes. Pap put his hand on her shoulder to comfort her.

Pap returned a glance to his office where he saw that his interaction with Alice had drawn the attention of Michael.

"Nothing to concern yourself with. She'll be alright. It's just that the priest in the paper performed her marriage to her late husband. He passed away a couple of years ago and I keep her here so she doesn't spend too much time worrying about being by herself. Her kids moved away a while ago and don't really keep up with her."

"That's horrible."

"Well, it's like that sometimes. Everyone who is related to you isn't necessarily your family.

Thankfully, there are enough people here who still look after one another which makes my job pretty easy. Now since it might not be a good idea for you to meander about in this town alone and in order to keep the relative ease of my occupation and calm of this town, you will be staying with me until your car is fixed. Even with Mr. Boone talking to those boys, it doesn't necessarily ensure that you will not be bothered."

Michael was looking forward to spending at least the next couple of nights in a rundown motel, complete with the years of forgettable patrons that had shared the same bed as he would. He thought about the way that all motel rooms smell of a mix of bleach, cigarettes, old perfume, mildew, and stale air. Despite the best efforts or even surface attempts, he always felt as though he could smell the last person to occupy the room. It was as if a cloud of their aroma and presence remained and waited for him to remind him that the room was not virgin territory.

When he first moved to Louisiana, he spent a fair share of nights in motels and two-star hotels. He was far from a connoisseur, but he knew what to expect when he arrived. There would always be someone at the front desk whose smile had been lost years prior to their meeting.

The air conditioning either didn't work or it worked too well, and he spent his stay sweating or freezing. There were some rooms where he didn't bother removing his shoes as he did not want to contract whatever viral infection had taken up residence in the carpet. He assuredly did not want to become patient zero in a global pandemic. The offer from Pap saved him from having to add another experience with haphazardly cleaned rooms and listening to the moans, yelling, or incessant coughing that could be heard through the paper-thin walls.

"Thank you."

"Hell, don't thank me just yet. We won't head out to my spot for another couple of hours. I still have to do a couple of rounds to complete and respond to some calls which means you'll be coming along for the ride or you could stay here and keep Alice company."

Michael looked out of the doorway and observed Alice who had returned to her slumber. Her head tilted back, and chin pointed over her shoulder. Her mouth was wide open, saliva trailing down the side of her face. There was nothing that appealed to Michael about this scene, not to mention, Alice had not risen once to make a pot of coffee, something that Michael had desired since sitting down with Pap at the Magnolia.

"So, Sheriff, is your couch a pull-out?"

Legal Aid

James drove off checking his phone for signs of life. Two bars appeared on the screen alerting him that he could successfully make a call. He quickly dialed the number for his attorney, Sterling Doucette.

After several rings, he was greeted by Sterling's voicemail.

"Sterling, this is James. Trip and Jody got into a bit of trouble last night, but I spoke to the Sheriff. Everything is probably ok, but I just need you to be prepared in case the guy they roughed up presses charges," he paused, taking in a deep sigh. "I also want to talk with you about amending my will. Call me when you get this. I don't care how late."

James waited for the tone signifying that his message had come to an end, but there was no notification. He pulled the phone away from his ear and saw that he had entered an area with no coverage.

He lay the phone in the seat next to him and continued down the road. His mind raced as he thought about the piece missing from his life for the past three decades. He had given up hope long ago, but today was different. It might be a long shot, but he would have to find out more about this young woman.

Brew Ha

Michael felt that the best course of action was for him to make the coffee himself. He grabbed the pot, washing it out in the sink before refilling the coffee maker with fresh water. Michael poured fresh grounds into the filter without having to measure. He flipped the switch and he waited as the water percolated. The aroma filled every pore of Michael's skin. The color returned to his face. His energy levels rose. Michael waited for the pot to brew in the same fashion as a child waits on the stairs Christmas Eve hoping to get a glimpse of Santa coming down the chimney to place presents under the tree. Michael had few vices. He had never done drugs despite all of the offers and opportunity in school. He wasn't a thrill junkie like some of his college friends who would go skydiving at the drop of a hat. He didn't even like to go too far above the speed limit. He always figured that rushing to a destination would increase the likelihood that you may not end up arriving at the destination.

Coffee was another thing altogether. It was his lifeblood. It was his companion for so many mornings and late evenings. It gave him the energy to write and research. It gave him that extra push each morning to subdue the thoughts of setting everything he owned on fire. On occasion, he was late to courses, faculty meetings, and committees all because the barista took too long to fill his order. He'd be damned if he were to talk about the finer points of American culture in the 1960s or budgets without a well-needed, and, in his opinion, well-deserved caffeine boost.

The coffee machine sang to him. The continued bubbling and dripping of the coffee into the pot filled Michael with joy. He grabbed one of the mugs from the counter and washed it out in preparation of this "gift from the Gods." He poured the contents of the pot into the mug he cleaned. The sounds of the coffee hitting the sides of the mug sounded as serene as waves crashing into the beach. It was pure tranquility. He wafted the smell of the coffee into his face, awakening every corpuscle in his nasal cavity. The events of the preceding night, the damage done to his car, and any other worry or concern was far from his mind. This magic brew had him under its spell.

As Michael put the rim to his lips, he heard the sound of a faint jingling. The jingling got louder. Michael ignored the sound as he allowed the muddy water to seep into his mouth. The nectar washed over his tongue. The man felt reborn. He felt anew. Michael conjured images of Popeye in his head being replenished and revitalized by spinach. He felt as though he could take on the roughnecks again after being refueled. Again, the jingling rang out. Michael's senses had grown stronger. He could no longer ignore the sound. He turned his head in the direction of it and saw Sheriff Pap shaking his keys by the doorway.

"You coming or not?"

Michael smiled, nodded, and walked out of the door behind Pap. He felt bulletproof.

Right Number, Wrong Person

Candice Boone sat in her white wicker chair as she furiously fanned herself to fend off the humid air as it approached her skin. Her mother's voice broke into her thoughts. "Ladies should never perspire. Whores perspire. Ladies glow."

The heat, most days, forced Candice to remain indoors, but she felt trapped when she avoided the elements by staying inside of her home. The stifling thick air may have been uncomfortable, but it didn't make her feel as she were captive.

The humidity had its benefits. Time slowed as it enveloped her. She watched as the world drifted by rather than racing forward as it seemed to have over the past five decades of her life.

The weight of her eyelids increased as she was consumed by the thick air. Candice's eyes shut, preparing her body to reject the reality and loneliness of the world. Tension had ceased to occupy her muscles. Her nerves were numbed. She lay her head back, increasing her level of comfort and drifted away. ELABORATE

Her peace was broken from the phone ringing inside. Candice was in no rush to answer it as she was so used to Gladys picking up the receiver before informing her or James who was on the other end of the line. As she sank down in her chair again, Candice was reminded that she had sent her to run errands. The thought of walking inside to answer the call was exhausting. She slowly rose from her seat to respond to the call if for no other reason than to return to the tranquility which had been broken by the ringing. As she reached out her hand to lift the receiver, the ringing stopped. The clicking of the answering machine started and she heard James' recorded voice.

"You have reached the Boone residence, please leave a message after the beep."

The long, drawn out beep that followed encouraged Candice to change directions and return to her chair on the porch. Within three steps of her trip, a shrill, angry voice filled the room.

"I've got a message for you, James Boone."

Candice walked back to the answering machine.

"Don't you ever step foot on my property again, you SON OF A BITCH!"

The answering machine stopped and the red light on the panel lit up with a "1."

Beads of perspiration ran down the back of Candice's neck. She knew that voice.

Eleanor!

Candice had gone out of her way to avoid any situation that would require her to interact with the likes of Eleanor. Eleanor was trash, plain and simple to someone like Candice. There was no need to dignify her existence. Candice glared at the blinking number one. She muttered under her breath and extended her hand to the receiver. She willed Candice to call back. She stared at the phone, waiting for it to ring. Her wish was granted as the trilling of the phone filled the room. Candice was incensed. Her face flushed as she lifted the receiver to her mouth.

"How dare you call my fucking home, you cheap whore?"

She was met with silence.

"HELLO?!?! You can call, but have nothing to say now?"

"Candice? This is Sterling. I was trying to reach James. I couldn't reach him on his cell. Is everything alright?"

"Oh. I am so sorry," she composed herself. "I just had a prank caller leaving the nastiest of messages."

"Sorry to hear that," he chuckled. Sterling never knew how to handle uncomfortable situations. "Well, just tell James I called. He left me a message at the office and I just needed some clarification before I draft these documents he was asking me about."

"Ok, I'll let him know that you called when he gets in."

Ride Along

Michael stared out of the window as the Sheriff drove around Laveau and St. Gerard Parish. He observed countless farms that grew cotton, sugar, rice, and livestock. Even with the pending sunset, the landscape was vivid. The color green filled his vision. Minutes would go by before he would see another soul outside.

Pap steered the vehicle down a gravel road. The crunching of the tires on the sharp rocks disturbed Michael. The grinding and popping made him feel as though the ground would open up under Pap's truck and swallow them leaving no signs of their existence behind. Pap, being quite familiar with the backroads of Louisiana was unmoved by the noise nor by Michael's countenance. The truck slid on each of the turns. If Michael had had anything other than the coffee that day, it surely would have been expelled from his body and onto Pap's dash. The zydeco music blared from the stereo with Pap singing along in French. Michael's mood changed as he tried to follow along with Pap's singing and the lyrics in the songs. This was unlike the French that he was required to take while in college. There was nothing formal about it. The words and usage broke numerous grammatical and linguistic rules that he abided when taking the courses. It wasn't long before he was tapping his feet to the music. His movements caught the attention of Pap.

"Ah, you like Zydeco?"

"This is my first time hearing it. It's catchy."

"Catchy? Shit. This music is responsible for anything from fucking to fighting. Half of the people in this state wouldn't exist if not for this," he said pointing at the radio.

"Where I'm from, it's whiskey that is usually at fault."

The truck continued winding down the gravel road before Pap veered off driving toward a small farmhouse. The sun was setting, and the headlights guided their voyage. Michael could hear the crickets and cicadas in the distance. It was a strange sound for him to hear. He was used to the cacophony of urban and suburban life. The silence was a bit unsettling for him. It added too much mystery. It reminded him that there was too much of the unknown in the darkness for him to be comfortable.

He had read about how people would go out into the woods and never be heard from again. He didn't want to be a statistic. Michael immediately thought about his emergency contacts and who would look for him if he wasn't heard from after several days. He couldn't think of anyone that he would trust enough to check up on him. He spoke to his parents roughly once a month. He had no significant other that would ensure that he was home by a reasonable time. With respect to work, he didn't teach on Fridays so no one would consider his absence on campus out of the norm. The weekend was approaching, and being the anti-social person that he was, he declined to make any plans with anyone. He looked at his phone and realized that there was no signal and his battery was nearly dead. "I'm fucked" he thought.

They pulled up to the home which was a small home with a mix of brick and white vinyl siding. The rose bushes outside needed trimming as their growth covered the front windows of the home and stretched toward the pathway of the door creating an obstacle for any and all visitors to the residence. As Pap but the vehicle in park, Michael questioned his role in this current situation. After all, he was simply waiting for Pap to complete his work for the day. He hadn't removed his seatbelt prompting Pap to give him an invitation.

"Come on out and stretch your legs. I just need to ask the old man a couple of questions. And don't slam my door," he said in a very direct but hushed tone.

Michael exited the vehicle taking to heart Pap's orders. He gently closed the door, however, his caution resulted in the door not fully closing. He reached through the window to unlock the door so that he could remedy his error. His action set off Pap's anti-theft alarm. The alarm rang out into the darkness. Pap threw a stern look at Michael before deactivating the system with his fob. With the siren off, the two men momentarily returned to the silence of the night.

The brief respite was broken by a loud gunshot. Michael ducked behind Pap's truck and peaked his eyes over the hood hoping to see where the shot rang from. He surveyed the scene to witness that Pap had not moved a muscle. He stood facing the house with one hand on his hip and the other with his thumb hooked inside of his front pant pocket. It was at that moment, he noticed that Pap was not carrying a side arm. *He's going to get himself killed*. Michael thought to himself.

He looked for an escape. There was nowhere but the darkness. The only bit of light was offered by the floodlights of the home. He would be damned if he went there. He wouldn't run to the darkness of the woods either. There was no refuge for him.

"Odysseus!" Pap yelled out.

Another shot rang out. Dirt flew up a few feet in front of Pap's feet.

"Pap, what are you doing?" Michael called out. "You are going to get yourself killed."

"Nah. He's eighty-four years old. He can't shoot for shit and he's half blind."

A third shot rang out causing more dirt and pebbles to jump off the ground yards away from where the previous shot landed.

"Odysseus!"

"Who owt der?" a voice called out from the house.

"It's Sheriff Pap."

"Sheet, Pap, dat's all you hadda say."

"Come on out, Odie. I need to talk to you about your car."

Michael, still cowering behind the truck looked over to see that Odie's carport was vacant. Pap did not make any of the details of their visit clear on the way to their destination. To him, this was a matter that could have easily been settled over the phone. It would have eliminated the chances of being shot by an old man in the middle of nowhere and Michael could be safe enjoying the comforts of air-conditioning.

"What 'bout mah cah?" The man yelled out from inside of his home.

"Well, your car was found flipped over on the side of the road outside of town."

"Whaddya mean mah cah was found outside of town? It ain ova der in the carpo?"

"Nah, Odie. It was found this morning. Your friend Jean-Baptiste was drunk and asleep in the passenger seat"

"He aight?" Odysseus asked.

"Yeah. He's going to be just fine. Folks at

the Bulldog saw the two of you drinking and cuttin' up last night"

"Dey ain see me, Pap. I was here all last night. Someone must have stole mah cah and gave Jean-Ba a ride home."

"Odie, come on out so we can talk."

"Ain dat wha weez doin' now, Pap? Besides, you wassin' time wid me when you should be out lookin' fo whoeva dun took mah cah."

"Alright, Odie," Pap said with a slight grin.

"Night, Pap."

Pap turned around and walked back to his vehicle. Michael's eyes widened. He was befuddled.

"What was that all about? It sounds like he was out drunk driving and almost got himself and his friend killed last night."

"Yeah. It do look like that don't it?"

"You're not going to arrest him?"

"What for? His friend Jean-Ba said damn

near the same thing when I went to see him at the hospital this morning. He said that he went out drinking and someone offered to give him a ride home. He didn't give me a name or a description."

"You can't do anything?"

"Not really. I go through this same routine with them almost every month. If one is not crashing their car, the other is. I don't have a warrant so I can't just barge in the man's home unless he lets me, or I catch him in the act. But since his friend is claiming the same thing, there is nothing I can do other than record it in the log. Besides, if I were to put everyone in jail for drinking and driving, the whole Parish would be locked up," Pap stated as he pulled out a small notepad and ballpoint pen, clicking it sharply, thus bringing an end to the conversation.

"Let's head on back to town. I could use a drink," he said as he climbed back into his truck. "You coming?"

Michael did not think long about his decision. He sat back down in the passenger seat. Remaining out here in the middle of nowhere was not a future he wanted to envision.

The two men rode off in the direction of

Laveau with talk radio now keeping them company. Michael thought about their interaction with Odysseus and he felt it gave him an opportunity to ask a question he was fearful of asking earlier.

"Sheriff, I've been meaning to ask."

"Shoot."

"I noticed that you don't carry a gun on you. Why?"

"Do you think I should?"

"Well no. That wasn't my reasoning. It's just that I've never seen, well outside of my travel to London, a police officer without one."

"Well, the issue for me is one I discovered years ago. My position is what gives me the authority in a situation and the way I carry myself and deal with people helps to control the situations I am called to. For me, I feel that if I am carrying a gun into any situation, I don't have the power or respect anymore. The gun does. There is no need for me to have a pistol on my hip. I do keep a shotgun and a rifle in the truck, but those have only been used to put down the rare rabid animal. It is not something I have had to use nor do I look forward to using. With this community, nearly everyone has had some contact with me, mostly positive, so when they see me, I have their respect."

"But what do you do if someone shoots at you?"

"Well, if it is anyone other than Odysseus, I duck."

Homecoming

James pulled his car into the garage. He sat there contemplating so many misdeeds and mistakes of his past. He had long questioned the meaning of his own life and why he felt joy evaded him despite the success he had in life. He looked at his hands and each crack in the skin, each spot told a story. They trembled as he inspected more deeply. The realization hit that he was no longer a young charmer. He was an old man, weathered by the trials and tribulations of life.

The skin on his hands was soft and fragile. The veins on his hands rose with each beat of his pulse, mimicking seconds ticking away on a clock. Each tick marked time that was running out in his life before it would be extinguished, and he would be little more than a memory.

He had no legacy in the form of progeny. Business, money, land, influence, it would all be gone upon his body returning to the earth. "Dust to dust," he said quietly as he turned the engine off.

James' father had died years ago, driving inevitability of death further into his mind. Reggie

Boone's shadow was one that James could never escape despite his best efforts. In life, his father never accepted anything but the best effort. He argued that one's best effort would result in success. If one fails to succeed it was due to them not working hard or putting their best foot forward. Even in death, James felt as though his father was looking over his shoulder, second guessing everything every action, decision, and thought that he ever had. The pain he felt in feeling that something was missing was immeasurable.

James had failed. He failed to have a legitimate heir that he could influence, teach, and teach. He was missing someone that he could connect with unlike any other person he would cross paths with. He didn't want a child to berate or mold into his own image. He knew the pain that his own father had caused to him and he sorely wanted to do something right with his life before it was over.

The door to the garage cracked open with the silhouette of a figure appearing behind the screened partition. "Are you just going to sit in here all night or are you going to come in and eat something?"

James nodded at the figure and exited the vehicle. James crept up to the door awash in a palpable melancholy. He said nothing. He made no sound aside from the heels of his shoes hitting the ground. He reached up to push a large button to lower the garage door. The grinding of the machinery gave him a brief jolt which broke him from his depressing mindset. James entered his home with his eyes and head lowered as he returned to this question of his existence. Something was missing. He did not feel whole. He walked in past the figure that had welcomed him home and sat down in his oversized recliner.

"Good evening, Candice," a voice called to him with a sarcastic tone.

"Huh?"

"I figured I should say it since you apparently missed your cue."

"I'm sorry, Candi. I just have a lot on my mind."

"That's no excuse to come home and not greet me, especially when you come home late without letting me know. Anyway, what is it that has your mind so occupied?"

"It's nothing, Candi. I'm just trying to put some ideas together, figure things out."

"Ok, well Gladys prepared a plate for you. It's in the kitchen."

"Thank you."

Candice looked down at him with complete contempt. He entered their home and sat in his chair, refusing to look at her as they talked. She didn't want to be near him, but she wanted to bring up the phone call from Sterling. It was certain that he would evade any question or possibly change the subject depriving her of any answers. There was no need to change his will in her mind. The only change that an amendment to the will would offer is removal of her or at least a reduction in what would be passed on to her in the event of his death.

Her mind raced as she evaluated every scenario as to why he would even push for any changes. There were no new business ventures that he had which would have prompted him to make changes. He hadn't sold nor acquired anything to her knowledge. *Maybe he was sick.* James hadn't been to the doctor recently which would prompt him to reevaluate his remaining time on Earth. *Maybe it was another woman.* He had been unfaithful to her in the past, each time she overlooked his missteps because of what it meant to be his wife. She was someone by marrying James. Her identity gained in prominence with her proximity to him. Being his wife offered unlimited privileges that went beyond wealth. She was not going to give that up willingly or passively. She'd be damned if she were to become a divorcee. Just the thought of her milling around town with other people pitying her brought chills to her skin.

She stood over him behind the chair and willed him to die in front of her. She wanted to see it. She needed to see him in agony. Seeing it would make her feel something besides the emptiness of their marriage. Candice smiled as she imagined how he would writhe on the floor in front of her begging for one more breath of air as he let out a "death rattle." She could see him bargaining with God for one more moment of life. The image of him gurgling out his last breath sexually aroused her. It was the first time anything related to his existence brought her close to climax.

"I'm heading on up to bed," she said as she kissed him goodnight on the top of his head.

"Goodnight," he replied to her,

halfheartedly.

Candice made the lonely walk to her bedroom. From the safety of her vanity, she removed the makeup that continued the charade that she carried on with herself in her attempt to deny the changes that time and nature had brought to her. Looking in the mirror, each wrinkle became more present. Each line in her face was more pronounced. The most disturbing blemishes were the ones that had formed around her mouth.

She sat down in the chair in front of her vanity as she continued wiping off the protective shield she had constructed so she could face the world. Each wipe of the cloth added a year. Each motion of her hands revealed an older woman as if it were a sadistic magic trick. The pictures around the room mocked her. Each was filled with, from an outsider's perspective, happy times, joyful experiences, love, and peace.

The images angered her, especially considering the tension that the phone call had brought into her home earlier that day. James' silence didn't help matters. Even if he were willing to talk, Candice was not ready for whatever he would say to her about the matter.

She turned each frame face down to where the only image in the room was the one staring back at her from the mirror. Despite the wrinkles, fine lines, and discoloration, she was filled with a burning sense of energy she had not felt for years. It was pure, unmitigated fury and hatred. She didn't deny or try to suppress it. She didn't question it internally.

A tube of red lipstick lay on the counter next to the towel she had just used to clean the makeup off her face. She picked it up and applied the color to her lips. Smiling, she moved closer to the mirror, placing a kiss on its surface. She rose and climbed into her bed, awaiting James to heed the call to slumber. It had been years since the two of them had shared a bed. Candice grew tired of having James come to bed late at night for various reasons. She was equally tired of having him wake her up early in the morning when he would leave to begin the day.

The years of her being a kept woman had culminated into her living a semi-single existence. The only person that she talked to on a regular basis in their home was their maid, Gladys. Talking would be an exaggeration of the term. Candice gave her instructions, would, on the occasion, ask about Gladys' family or various plans, but there was nothing of depth. Gladys was a thing to her, not a full person. Saying that she thought that this woman was equal even to a minimum of 3/5s would be a stretch. Candice, when learning about aspects of history in her youth, always seemed to miss the important lessons that conflicted with her privileged position in the world. If it didn't matter to her, it simply did not matter at all. Why should she concern herself with those that she saw as being lower than she was?

Whispers

Downstairs, James poured himself a glass of bourbon. He thought that alcohol may be the best companion for him to think about his exposure earlier in the day. *Who was she? Why did she seem so familiar to him? What was it about her that made her feel welcome and safe yet guilty?* He ran through his mind every possible conclusion as to why there was an air of confusion and certainty in the air surrounding her. With each sip, he slipped deeper into a vortex. He walked back to the chair with his glass in one hand and a bottle in the other. He continued drinking and contemplating. There was no resolution. All he had was her name.

As he became more relaxed in the chair, he was interrupted by the ringing of the phone beside him. He reached over and put the receiver to his ear.

"Hello?"

"James! Is everything alright? I normally wouldn't call you at home this late, but the message you left for me seemed a bit off. I just wanted to clarify it."

In a surly tone James responded.

"What is so confusing about wanting to amend my will?"

His voice disturbed his bride who had just closed her eyes upstairs. She rose out of the bed and walked to her door. She slowly opened it in the hopes of catching more of the conversation. Everything was muffled now that James was speaking in a normal tone. Candice looked to her nightstand which held her phone. She inched her way to the handset hoping that it would alleviate her desire to be informed on the night's proceedings. She gingerly lifted the received, covering the mouthpiece to ensure that she could not be heard on the other end. Her pupils dilated at being able to satiate her hunger to discover what James was talking about, and more importantly, who he was talking to.

Who was it? Was this why he was coming in so late and has nothing to say to me?

"James, everything will be just fine. You can come by my office on Monday."

Candice let out a sigh. She was comforted to hear that it was a man's voice on the phone. It was business. It was uneventful, boring, and did not present a further need for her to worry that it was the woman who had called earlier. The anger and vitriol in the woman's voice made Candice concerned that this woman might show up in the dead of night. She continued listening.

"Look, I know that you are busy, but you are my attorney and I would expect that if I needed something as simple as an amendment to my will made, it could be done."

"It's not a problem. The issue is that there are forms that I have to prepare, and I can't just simply make the changes that you want on my legal pad. There is procedure involved. If it will make you feel better, we can meet at my office tomorrow over lunch."

"That could work."

"Thank you, Sterling."

The conversation ended as both men hung up their phones. Candice was still holding onto the receiver in her bedroom, her mind a brewing storm of confusion, contempt, and feeling betrayed.

Why did James want to change anything about his will?

She was on the chopping block. Louisiana was a community property state, but James' lawyer could draw up papers that would leave her with nothing more than her name and the clothes on her back. Candice wanted it all. She knew that she was the only one who deserved it. She would not be denied nor forgotten.

Candice hung up the receiver and drew the sheets back over her body. She could not rest. She questioned what the full meaning of the conversation was. She sat up and allowed her mind to race. She allowed it to wander. As thought compounded on thought, she dragged her psyche through a multitude of scenarios and possibilities, none of which were positive or beneficial for her. James had been unfaithful to her in the past only for her to forgive him each time. She was done forgiving him, especially after the earlier call that day.

The blank wall she stared into became a canvas that presented an amalgamation of colors and voices. She could hear women and men conspiring against her. She heard James' laughter. Her own screams and distraught filled her head. She imagined herself walking the streets alone, haggard, dirty, and feeling onlookers revile and pity her. She had no choice. She would not be a victim to life and circumstance. Survival was her focus now. She was wounded. Candice knew that there was nothing more dangerous on Earth than a wounded animal. She was going to make sure that the pain she had was felt by those responsible for the agony she was overcome with. Candice was a survivor.

The solitude and emptiness of the room magnified her isolation. Candice pulled her sleep mask over her eyes to dull the pain of being alone in the room. Despite the coolness of the room and the comfort of the bed, she still could not rest. She slowed her breathing and concentrated on the nothingness that met her on the inside of the mask covering her eyes. It was black, cold, and empty. She began to drift away.

A Kiss Goodnight

Candice's heart raced so loudly that she thought it could be heard outside of her body. She placed her hand over her chest to muffle the depth to which her heartbeat. She slowed her breathing in a vain attempt to alleviate the anxiety. She slowly and quietly pushed the door open to James' bedroom. She slithered forward and saw him lying face down on his bed. Her eyes narrowed. She saw nothing in that chamber other than the man she had married and come to despise. There was no color. There was no sound other than the blood coursing through her veins. The taste of ash overcame her mouth. She approached the bed.

Candice carefully climbed on top of James, putting her knees over his outstretched arms. She imagined herself as a praying mantis killing her mate. When she was young, she thought the idea of a creature killing their partner was unimaginable. Years of marriage had made her understand that call to snuff out the life that had been intertwined with hers.

James had not moved despite Candice putting every ounce of her weight of him. She sat perched on his back and arms, waiting to strike.

She could feel his breath enter and exit his body as his torso expanded. She wanted to hear that gurgle. She wanted him to die in front of her but couldn't dare face him. James had made her mission possible with his positioning on the bed. She stared into the back of his head; the blonde hair having turned white years ago. Cautiously, she grabbed one of the oversized pillows that lay next to James on the bed. Candice raised the casing full of feathers and padding over her head. Her breathing stopped. Her heartbeat was faint. She lowered the pillow and rested it to her side. This was not the way she wanted things to conclude.

Candice held her hands in front of her face. They were steady. Her mind was unwavering. She turned her hands palms down and pressed down on the back of James' head with all the effort she could muster. James' body came alive. He began to writhe. His voice was muffled as his face was pressed down into the mattress. He could not call out for help. He could not move. Candice, despite her small figure, rendered him immobile as she sat on his arms and back. He could not escape. James was her prey and she was not going to allow him to get away. She groaned and grunted as she pushed his head harder into the bed. She kept her eyes on the back of his head. She rejoiced at seeing what her hands were capable of. She had never been prouder. She never felt more alive. She wanted to finish him. She wanted to hear his last breath exit his body. She wanted to be in control for the first time since she could remember. The only other death she was responsible for was by accident. This one was of her own design.

She pressed against James' head until she could feel her veins protrude from her arms. Her fingers were fatigued and sore, yet she continued. She felt tears stream from her eyes and down her face. Her face hurt. Candice caught a glimpse of herself in the dresser mirror. She was smiling. She smiled back at the distorted figure that she caught in the aged reflection. She found joy. She felt powerful. She was in control. She was beautiful.

Candice looked down at James' body. He had ceased to move. There was no palpable breathing. She pulled his head back to see his eyes were closed. She climbed off him and descended from the bed. Candice backed away quietly from the remnants of her husband. It was almost too easy, she thought. She questioned why she had not done it years earlier. There was no shame in the deed. There was no room in her mind to find herself at fault. James needed to be removed and she gave no more consideration to it than if he had been an ant crawling around in her kitchen. He was gone. She was free.

"Goodnight, James," she whispered, blowing him a kiss as she closed the door.

Awakenings

Images of James' dead body filled Candice's mind. She was overwhelmed with them. Each one was more grotesque and morbid than the last. She smiled thinking about him being gone. She was free.

Candice saw James laid out in a casket, perfumed, with makeup on, and his eyes closed made him look as though he were simply sleeping. His blue suit fit perfectly. Something about the way that he was presented in the gold-trimmed casket made him look younger than she could remember. He looked, to her, like that young boy she chased, and was chased by, around town when she was a teenager. She saw herself crying over the casket as throngs of sympathetic visitors expressed their sorrow for her loss. She sat down, needing to rest from the stress of seeing him and having to hear from each attendant about how sorry they were for her loss. She could not escape the room or the atmosphere. It would be in bad taste for the widow to be absent.

With each passing person, the faces disappeared. They were all a blur in front of her face. The voices mixed together and drowned out any discernable words. Conversations were taking place, but she took no part. The room became stifling. Her airway was constricted. She stood to get away from the crowd of guests to be with James one more time. As she stood over the casket, she looked down upon her dearly departed. The youthful face that she saw moments earlier was gone. What met her was a frail, wrinkled, gray, and rotting corpse. His hazel eyes were replaced by empty, black holes.

Candice recoiled at the sight of the body. As she took a step back, she was met by the hands of those who came to comfort her. She was being grabbed by the hands of half a dozen attendees. She tried to swat them away. With each attempt, Candice found more hands on her body.

"We know," they said in an eerie unison.

She turned around to face them only to discover no one behind her. Candice felt the guilt of her actions compound with the voice. A chill ran down her spine. She took a step back but was obstructed by the casket. Startled with the abrupt stop to her escape, she turned to face the casket again. It was empty. Candice grabbed the satin pillows and liner as she struggled to find James.

"Candi?" James' voice called out behind her.

Cold sweat beaded on her brow. She closed her eyes. Candice did not want to see James' face again. She thought he was dead. His body was in the casket. It was rotting. The flesh was pulling away from the bone. She moved closer to his remains. His skin had dissolved into ashes. Only his bones remained.

"Candi?" his voice called out from the casket.

She couldn't speak. Her lips quivered and her eyes darted. There was nothing but darkness surrounding her. She closed her eyes again.

"Candi?" the voice called, prompting her to open her eyes once more. James' remains were sitting upright in the casket. The skull turned to face her. A finger pointed in her direction. The bony hand moved closer to her. Candice was paralyzed with fear. The hand crept closer.

"Candi?" The voice called out as the jaw of the skull dropped to the floor and shattered upon impact.

Candice stepped away from the casket. She turned, looking for an exit, but found none. Candice reached her hands out in vain hoping to find a door to save her from this terror. There was no escape, no sanctuary, no refuge.

She rubbed her hands together out of fright and frustration.

"This is hell. I am in Hell!"

Two hands grasped her shoulders and crept up her neck. Candice turned to break from the grasp of her captor. She looked at her foe. A woman stood in front of her in a white wedding gown. Under the veil, Candice could see that her eyes were weeping blood. Her wrists were slit. The woman had a bloody mass in her chest where her heart would be. She stepped closer to Candice who was frozen in her spot. No words came out of her mouth. Candice's breathing had stopped. The woman put her hands around Candice's neck again and in a faint, raspy voice uttered, "You did this to me. These are your sins. You did this to me."

Candice stretched her arms out to repel the assault. She flailed her arms and fingers as she tried to grab some part of the woman in front of her. Her hand hooked onto the woman's veil. Candice pulled her hand back, bringing the veil with it. The woman's head sunk into her chest with her hair draped over her face. Candice continued to fight the woman's grasp. She lifted her head, revealing her face. The face of her attacker was her own.

Candice ripped her sleep mask off and sat up in bed. She pulled her knees into her chest and began sobbing. She looked at her hands. She was not fearful. She was enraged. Candice covered her face with her hands and allowed reality set back into her mind.

Night Calls

James brought the glass to his lips to finish off the remaining bourbon. The smoky flavor danced on his tongue and relaxed him further. After setting the glass down on the end table, he rose to call and end to the evening and wish good riddance to a complicated and hectic day. He loosened the laces on his shoes before taking them off. With Candice asleep, he did not dare risk waking her with the hard soles of his oxfords hitting the wood stairs. Each step with those shoes sounded like a smack which was amplified by the abundant space in their home.

The clinking sound of the ice hitting the inside of a glass downstairs snapped Candice out of her moment of self-pity. She rose from the bed and approached her bedroom door with a clear plan forming in her mind. James would not live to see another sunrise.

James reluctantly approached the stairs. He wanted the day to end so his mind could be at ease. He looked forward to starting a new day with a clear head where he could seek out answers to the questions circling his mind.

She opened the door slightly. Her eyes

peered toward the staircase where she witnessed James gingerly ascending the stairs. He had one hand on the railing and the other was occupied with his glass. With each step, Candice plotted her next move.

James reached another step.

Now is the time! She thought to herself.

Candice exited the doorway and crept toward the landing. A slight curl formed at the corner of her mouth as she fought off a smile. James briefly lost his balance and spilled a bit of his drink on the steps. Leaning forward, he gripped the handrail to regain his equilibrium. As he steadied himself, he raised his head to discover how much of his journey remained. Counting the stairs, his eyes caught sight of Candice.

"Did I wake you?" he asked with concern and slightly slurred.

"Oh no. I've been awake for a while," she coldly replied.

James approached the landing and stood facing Candice.

"Goodnight, Candi."

He leaned forward in an attempt to kiss her but was promptly rebuffed as she leaned away from his advance.

"What is it?"

Candice wanted to fight the urge to ask the question that had been plaguing her, but it was a lost cause as she heard the words emerge from her own mouth.

"Who?"

Candice's temper started to rise. She clenched her teeth and wrung her hands.

"Who… is… she?"

"Candi, what are you talking about?"

His denial infuriated her more.

"You came in late and didn't answer your phone earlier. Sterling called here looking for you. What am I supposed to think?"

She angrily pushed against his chest with her index finger.

"Candice, you are being ridiculous."

He tried to pass, but she blocked his path.

"Let me by."

"Let you by? I've let you *get by* all these years. I am not a pushover nor am I a doormat. You won't knock me down or walk over me anymore."

"You are talking crazy" He said as he laughed and raised the glass to his lips.

Dejected, Candice slapped the glass out of his hand. James' drink spilled down his face and onto his shirt before crashing to the floor.

"Goddammit, Candice!" James yelled as he took a step back to wipe his face. "Shit! I need to get a towel and something to pick up all of this broken glass."

James turned his back to Candice as he surveyed the mess.

Candice lunged forward toward James.

"We're not done here!"

She misjudged the force of her hands and small frame. Her momentum propelled James forward. His attempt to grab the handrail failed. James tumbled down the stairs three steps at a time. The first snap heard marked the breaking of his wrist. The second snap was of his right leg. The third was his neck.

James slid down the remaining steps on his back, leaving a bloody trail, before coming to a rest at the bottom of the stairs. His lifeless eyes remained open. His life had been extinguished. Candice looked down upon him with a smile. She walked backed to her room and climbed back into her bed. Her skin was flushed. She felt electricity pass through her extremities. She smiled, catching a glimpse of herself in the mirror. The excitement of the night's events made her feel reborn.

Chez Pap

Sheriff Pap pulled the truck into his driveway and came to a stop in his carport. He slapped Michael on the arm, waking him.

"Home sweet home."

Michael wiped his eyes before checking the time on his watch.

11:13

"Come on. Let's get you settled."

In the haze of his still weary mind, Michael smirked as he thought about the irony of getting "settled" after quite an unsettling day. He exited the truck and followed Pap. Pap's keys jingled as he turned them in the lock. The two men walked through a doorway into a pitch-black room. To Michael, it felt like entering an abyss.

In the darkness, Michael heard the flick of a switch. The room immediately illuminated, transforming the space from a cold, barren void into a colorful, warm, and welcoming environment.

"Make yourself comfortable, Mike."

Michael's eyes were drawn to the leather sofa across from him. He sat down and eyelids sank.

"I have to apologize. I don't have guests too often. Between that and work, I don't really have much to offer you, so if you get hungry, your options are slim and none," Pap said from down the hall while digging through the closet for a blanket and pillow.

"That's quite alright. I can wait until morning," he replied with a yawn.

Pap returned with an old olive drab army blanket and a pillow without a case under his arm.

"This should get you through the night," he said to Michael who was now fast asleep.

Pap gently put the blanket on top of Michael and sat in his recliner. He turned the television on in the hopes of catching *SportsCenter.* Before long, Pap's head sunk into his chest as he joined Michael in the world of slumber.

The Dead Can't Hear You

"Hey, we need to go," Pap said as he shook Michael awake.

"What happened?" Michael responded, startled.

"James Boone is dead. Fell down the stairs and broke his neck. Dr. Benavides is already down there. He asked me to come by and console Boone's wife and to have the death officially recorded. The maid found the body this morning and both she and Ms. Boone are inconsolable."

Michael squirmed at the idea of death almost as much at the thought of seeing a dead body. He avoided funerals. He found them to be a spectacle and a fruitless endeavor. There was no point in fawning over someone's remains. The dead couldn't see those in attendance, nor could they hear the prayers said over their bodies. The most ridiculous thing about the whole event was the idea that everyone in attendance had nothing but the best to say about the departed. Everyone who ever existed was a dedicated spouse, loving parent, or devoted friend. It was all bullshit to Michael. The words spoken at those funerals were rarely stated while the person was among the living. Despite his feelings on the matter and his discomfort, Michael followed Pap out of the door.

Death Comes For Us All

Sheriff Pap guided his truck down the long tree-lined driveway that led to the Boone residence. Michael marveled at the immense trees whose branches reached out to the road to grab those who would pass by. He sunk deeper into his seat as he imagined being snatched up by one of the oak, pine, and magnolia giants that loomed over him.

Pap pulled next to the hearse that had been sent over from the Doucette funeral home. Michael grew nauseous at seeing the black vessel of death. Michael cautiously exited Pap's truck, passing slowly by the hearse as to avoid the specter of death he feared would emerge from the back of the vehicle. He held his breath and shielded his eyes as he approached Sheriff Pap who was speaking with Dr. Benavides on the front steps of the residence.

"You alright there, Dr. Dubs?"

"Yeah. I'm good," he replied as he focused on the bridge of Pap's nose.

"It is a good thing that the body has already been wheeled off and in that hearse because it is too early for me to be picking you up off the ground from fainting at the sight of a dead man."

"It's not that. I just have this thing about the idea of death."

"Everybody does. Hey, why don't you keep Dr. Benavides company while I go check on Ms. Boone. I shouldn't be long."

Sheriff Pap disappeared through the large entryway where the new widow was burying her face in a lavender handkerchief.

Michael's heart sank as he thought about the loss and despair that this woman was undergoing. He turned to look back at the hearse and saw a white sheet covering what used to be James Boone. Less than 24 hours earlier, he was having a conversation with the man. He looked to be in good health. He carried himself as someone who took care of himself and free of health concerns.

"Death comes for us all, eventually," Dr. Benavides said with his gravelly voice.

"What happened?" Michael asked under his breath.

"He fell," Dr. Benavides responded.

"Oh, I'm sorry. I didn't think I said that aloud."

"Not a problem, son. I'm not violating anyone's confidence of privacy. Apparently, he fell down the stairs and broke his neck. I found some broken glass at the top of the stairs. It looks like he was enjoying a nightcap, headed to bed, and probably lost his balance. I can't imagine what is going on through that poor woman's mind. They've been together nearly forty years."

"My whole life," Michael whispered.

"Funny you say that. He was the only person in hers. I'm glad Pap showed up when he did. I am not known for my bedside manner. I was just praying that he or Father Riley would show up to relieve me before I stuck my foot in my mouth and made things even more uncomfortable. I haven't met you before. You just start working for Sheriff Pap?"

"Oh no," Michael tripped over his words. "Well, it's a long story."

"In that case, don't worry about it. Long stories are typically problematic, and I have enough on my plate this weekend."

Pap emerged from the house approaching Michael and Dr. Benavides.

"I think she'll be alright, considering. Doc, you need anything from me?"

"No Pap. We're good here. The body is loaded up. We just need to drop him off at the funeral home."

"Well," Pap said as he placed his sunglasses back on. "let's go get something to eat."

A Brave Façade

Candice stared out of the window as she watched her visitors depart. Her tears dried up and her frown transformed into a smile. Her ruse had worked. No one suspected that she had snuffed out James' life. Candice walked to the window and watched as the hearse and Pap's truck became smaller and smaller as they approached the horizon. She stood in silence as they disappeared through the line of trees that led out to Laveau.

"Mrs. Boone, are you sure you're ok?" Gladys asked as she cautiously walked up behind Candice.

"I'm fine, dear. Just fine. You go on and head home. Thank you for being here for me, but I think I need to be alone right now."

"If you need anything, please call me," Gladys said as she grabbed Candice's hand. "Don't you worry, Mr. Boone is in God's hands now."

Candice nodded and pulled the handkerchief up to her eyes, feigning tears.

"Bless you."

Gladys departed, leaving Candice in the foyer of her home, all alone. She shut and locked the door behind Gladys. Candice turned, facing the stairs as she made her way back to her room. As she approached the steps, she felt a chill. Goosebumps formed on her arms, forcing her to end her journey. She looked at the base of the stairs where James' life had come to an end. She smirked as she looked over the spot. Candice swished saliva around in her mouth and spat on the floor where his body once lay.

"God's hands?"

Candice grabbed the phone on the table at the base of the stairs and slowly dialed the number for James' attorney. She caught a glimpse of herself in the hallway mirror and returned to her façade.

"Hello?" the voice answered.

"Sterling, James passed last night. Gladys found him at the bottom of the stairs this morning."

"I'm sorry Candice. Are you ok? Is there anything I can do for you?"

"Thank you, Sterling. You have always been a good friend to James. He told me that he wanted to add someone to his will. I want to make sure that his wishes were honored."

"Oh yes. He and I were talking about that yesterday. He was supposed to meet with me today in order to go over the amendments, but he never told me who he specifically wanted to add or remove as a beneficiary."

"Eleanor Deschamps. He told me earlier this week that they were friends as children, and he wanted to make sure that she was taken care of. Do you mind calling her so we can set everything up legally? I have to meet with the funeral home to set up James' service."

"Of course. I can't begin to imagine how stressful this day has been for you. Let's meet around 6 at my office. That should give you more than enough time to meet with the funeral director and the church."

"Thank you, Sterling. I'll see you then."

Candice hung up the receiver before Sterling could reply.

The ideas began to spin in her head. The first step toward her freedom had been achieved. She had one more to take ensuring that no threat remained.

Beneficiary

Sterling thumbed through his contact list finding Eleanor's phone number. After one ring, a warm voice greeted him.

"Hello?"

"Ah, yes. I am trying to reach Eleanor Deschamps."

"Sure, may I ask who's calling?"

"Yes, ma'am. This is Sterling Doucette."

"Just a sec." Vanessa covered the receiver as she relayed the message to her mother. Eleanor sat across from her at the bar enjoying her coffee with chicory and reading the paper. She pulled her reading glasses off her nose and let them hang from their chain around her neck. A puzzled look formed on her face.

"What in the Holy Fuck does he want with me?"

"Well, mama, you could take the phone and find out for yourself," smiled Vanessa. "Here she comes now Mr. Doucette," She cheerfully said into the phone.

"Give me that damned thing" Eleanor groaned as she snatched the phone away from her daughter.

"Eleanor," she curtly grumbled into the phone.

"Afternoon, ma'am. I'm Sterling Doucette and I represent the estate of James Boone."

"Estate?" Eleanor was confused.

"Yes ma'am. James Boone passed this morning and it was brought to my attention that he recently expressed his wishes to add you as a beneficiary, but we did not have the opportunity to officially make the amendments before he passed."

Sterling continued talking, but Eleanor hadn't heard a word after Sterling informed her of the passing of Boone. Her skin flushed as she found joy in receiving the news. She never liked James and tried as much as possible throughout her life to ensure that their paths never crossed.

"I hate to inconvenience you, but can you come down to my office this evening around six in order to sign the paperwork and have this recorded?"

"At six on a Saturday?"

"Yes ma'am. The family requested the time. They are meeting with the funeral directors and church to go over the service. Mrs. Boone assured me that she should be done by that time in order to meet with us and approve the amendments to have you included."

"I don't know."

"I assure you that I will not take up too much of your time. I am drafting the paperwork now and I shouldn't need anything other than a couple of signatures. It's a fairly pain-free process."

Eleanor paused, holding the receiver to her chest, watched her daughter behind the bar before returning to the conversation.

"Six?"

"Yes ma'am. My office is at 300 North Jefferson Boulevard."

"I'll see you then." She hung up the phone before returning to her coffee.

Eleanor knew that even a small percentage of the Boone Estate would ensure that she never had to worry about Vanessa's future.

Appetite

Pap and Michael sat at the counter of Hal's Diner before being greeted by a smiling silver-haired woman.

"Good morning, Pap," she said as she poured a freshly brewed cup of coffee for the Sheriff.

"Morning, Verna," he replied as he placed his hat on the seat to his left.

"And Good morning to you, hun," she said as she turned to Michael. "What can I get for you?"

"Oh, I'll have some coffee to start with."

"You've been quiet this morning," Pap casually stated as he sipped his coffee.

"It's nothing. I just don't handle death well."

"Look, if you handled death well, I might be a little uneasy being alone in a car with you. Hell, I'd second guess having you to continue staying in my house."

Pap ordered for them both. He talked to Michael about elements of his life. Michael nodded, only taking in every other word while his mind was focused elsewhere. The only thing that stopped Pap from giving Michael his own history was the arrival of the food.

Michael watched as Pap unrelentingly ate his pecan waffles with extra syrup, two cups of coffee, eggs, bacon, and grits. He watched with an uneasy stomach, wondering how Pap could be some comfortable in light of just coming from the scene of someone's death.

Pap looked up as he polished off his plate to see that Michael hadn't touched his food.

"You know. If you aren't hungry, we can have them pack it up for you so you can eat it at my office."

Pap signaled to Verna that he was done and would need a box. She quickly came over, packed the meal.

The two men exited the diner in completely different moods and dispositions. Pap happily walked to the truck while Michael's feet dragged, giving him more of an undead appearance. The two sat back down in the truck. Pap clapped his hands together, briefly shocking Michael, "Let's roll!"

Crimson Smile

Eleanor reluctantly walked to her car thinking about the absurdity of James Boone adding her to his will, but she was comforted in knowing that it wasn't about her. This was about ensuring a better life for Vanessa. Eleanor would sell her soul to make a future possible for her. She often regarded James as the devil incarnate so swallowing her pride over this issue wouldn't be far off from an eternal contract with the actual antichrist.

Her head swam with thoughts about what awaited her when she arrived at Sterling Doucette's office. She was quickly brought back down to Earth as she remembered that she needed to make this process as quick as possible so she could return and open the Magnolia that evening. Eleanor didn't like being away from her business, especially on the weekends.

As she sat in the car, she looked around and saw that there were no other vehicles outside of the building. She looked at the building to ensure that she was at the correct address.

300 North Jefferson Boulevard

She was in the correct place.

Looking at her watch she sighed and sat back in her seat. She was early and she feared the other arrivals would be late. Eleanor hated waiting on people. She had learned the importance of time at an early age. Her focus on punctuality was so strict that she viewed arriving on time as being late.

She checked her watch again

5:55

Eleanor stepped out of her car and approached the building. All the windows were dark. The only noise she could hear was the birds chirping and a gentle rustle of leaves as the winds passed through the trees. Eleanor put her hands around her eyes as she pressed her face against one of the windows, hoping to gain a glimpse of some life inside. There was nothing. It was the weekend, after all, and Sterling could be inside by himself. She grabbed her cell phone and called the office number listed on the door. She walked around the building as she waited for someone to pick up on the other end. There was no answer. As she found herself on the backside of the building, she rang the doorbell with the faint hope that someone would respond.

Eleanor checked her watch again, seeing that it was now one past the hour. She sat back down in her car and wrapped her hands around the wheel nervously tapping her thumbs on the worn leather. There was no one around and no cars were approaching.

"Fuck this," she said, looking at the front door of the building through the windshield.

Eleanor picked up her phone to call Vanessa and let her know she was on her way home.

As she looked up in the rearview mirror to back out of the space, she was surprised by a hand covering her mouth with a cloth and her seatbelt being wrapped around her neck. She struggled and clawed at her attacker, reaching behind herself. Eleanor tried to grab hair, an ear, anything that could stop the assault, dropping her phone to the floorboards in the process. All her attempts failed. She felt her eyelids drop and her breath fainter. She could hear her pulse slow and fade. The last thing she saw was a crimson smile and lipstick covered teeth.

"You bi...."

Lifeline

Pap pulled his truck up to the front steps of the Magnolia. Carl was perched outside on a stool reading a worn copy of *Harry Potter and the Sorcerer's Stone.* Without looking up from the pages, he greeted the new arrivals.

"Morning, Pap."

"Morning Carl," he returned as he casually walked up the steps. "You reading that again?"

"Yeah, Pap. I love this shit. Ever since my little girl could read, she has been all about wizards, witches, and magic. Plus, I know reading this pisses off all the churchgoing folk. I can't wait for the next movie comes out about Magical Beasts. Y'all go on in." He waved his hand at the door and stated "Alohomora."

Michael gave him a strange, confused look.

"Latin?" he asked.

"Nah. Just seeing if any of this would work in the real world."

Pap and Michael passed to enter. As they crossed the threshold, they could hear Carl mutter, "Damn muggles."

Sitting behind the bar was Vanessa enjoying an iced coffee and reading *Native Son*. She turned her book facedown to welcome the men.

"Hey, Pap," she said as she stretched across the bar to give the Sheriff a kiss on the cheek.

"Hey, Doc. What are the two of you up to?"

"Not much, sweetheart," Pap replied. "It's been quite an eventful day."

"How so?" she asked, pouring the two men glasses of tea.

"Well, James Boone died last night. His wife discovered his body this morning."

"Wow. What happened?" Her eyes grew larger. "Was he sick or something?"

"He apparently fell down the stairs late last night at home."

"That's horrible," she stated, covering her heart. "Is his wife okay?"

"As good as anyone can expect."

"I was on my way to check on her again after I stopped by here to see if y'all needed anything."

"We should be good to go for tonight, but with Mr. Boone passing, I doubt will be too busy."

"Where's your mama at?"

"You just missed her. She left out of here a while ago but didn't say where she was going. I figured that she probably had some man she didn't want me knowing about."

"Oh, so she's cheating on me now?" Pap chuckled.

"Let me call and see where she is." Vanessa pulled her cell phone out of her purse and pushed the button to autodial her mother's number. There was no answer. "Nothing Pap. I'm just getting her voicemail."

"No problem, just give me a call if you need anything."

Pap turned to exit with Michael in tow.

"Thank you for the tea."

As the two men made it to the truck, Vanessa burst through the door startling Carl.

"PAP!!!" she screamed, holding up a cordless phone.

"What is it?"

"Pap, I don't know. It's mama... I don't...."

Vanessa was hysterical and could not catch her breath. Her voice cracked and her hands were shaking.

"What is it, girl?"

"Pap, listen. Listen to it Pap."

He took the phone out of her trembling hands.

Pap hastily put the receiver to his ear.

All Pap could hear was what sounded like rustling, thumping, and muffled speech. Then a voice cut through the static.

You bitch! You're not taking anything from me. I killed him and I won't stop from killing you, too. You are going to tell me why... why I have to lose everything because of you.

"Michael, stay here!"

"What's going on?" Michael looked back

and forth between Pap and Vanessa.

"Pap, I'm coming with you!" Vanessa yelled as she approached Pap's truck.

"The hell you are. You are staying here." He stuck his head out the driver's side window. "Carl, she doesn't step one foot off this property. Ya hear?"

"Sure thing, Pap." He said without looking up from his book.

"I'm fucking serious!" Pap yelled as he pulled away from the building. He turned and sped off so quickly, his tires shot gravel at the trees and building as he drove away from the Magnolia.

The voice terrified Pap, and that was no easy feat.

Tears welled up in Vanessa's eyes. "I have to go."

"But Pap." Michael attempted to dissuade her.

"She is going to kill my mother!" Vanessa yelled, gritting her teeth.

"Who?"

"I don't know, but I heard her voice."

Vanessa spun around and burst through the doors. Carl was unbothered. Michael stood in silence, not knowing what to do. Vanessa emerged from the building with her car keys in one hand and a pistol in the other.

"We're closed for tonight Carl!" she said as she ran down the steps.

"Okay," he said, licking his finger to turn another page.

"But Sheriff Pap…" Michael interjected.

Carl pointed his index finger at Michael and calmly said "obliviate."

Michael was dumbfounded.

"You should probably go with her, I'm still on the clock."

Be Just

Pap's foot pressed the accelerator nearly through the floor. The growl of the engine equaled the anxiety he felt in his chest. The voicemail filled him with a fear he had not experienced since he first took over as Sheriff. He thought about the dead woman he came upon less than six months into his first term. He had never seen a dead body other than attending a funeral. He could still smell the blood. He could still see the disfigurement in her face. His mind forced images of Eleanor's face on the woman's body. Death had a different meaning when it was someone close. Pap prayed that he would find Eleanor before it was too late. He clearly heard Candice's voice in the messages. She sounded like a woman possessed.

Where could they be?

He knew everyone in the Parish and all of their secrets, yet he couldn't imagine where Candice could be or where she could be taking Eleanor. He drove to the first place that made sense: The Boone residence. Pap drove down the long driveway only to see Sterling Doucette seated outside of the entryway.

"Sterling! Where is Mrs. Boone?" he yelled

from his truck.

"Don't know. She was supposed to be here for a meeting at six with Eleanor. I've been waiting here since quarter till. With her being so distraught, I just assumed that I should wait here. We were supposed to meet at my office, but she called and told me she would be more comfortable here. Hell, she even called Ms. Deschamps herself to reschedule the venue.

"Ok. If you see her, call me immediately and don't tell her that we have spoken," Pap said as he drove off.

He knew he had to backtrack and find some way to track down Candice before it was too late for Eleanor. He calculated the possible places where they could be.

Pap sped through Laveau, arriving at Sterling's office. No one was there. No cars sat outside of the building.

"Come on. Where are you?"

Pap knew that Candice wouldn't kill Eleanor in public or anywhere she could be seen. He ran down a list in his mind of any and all places.

Pap drove back toward his office. He was lost. He had no direction or idea of where to go. He sat at the roundabout that encircled the courthouse. The statue outside stood resolute. Every time he passed it, he was reminded why he chose to run for Sheriff by the words inscribed at its base.

Be Vigilant, Be Fearless, Be Just.

The monument held a book of laws under her right arm and a sword pointing west in her left hand.

"The church."

Pap sped off in the direction of St. Richard's. For him, this was the only place that made sense.

Darkness and Light

As he approached the church, he slowed his vehicle. He scanned the grounds, hoping to see one of the women, if not both. He wanted to see something, anything that would signify their presence. Next to the church he saw Eleanor's car. Pap pulled his truck next to the vehicle and scanned inside. There was no one inside. He drove his truck around the church and saw movement in the graveyard behind the church. He pointed his spotlight in the direction of the figure he saw.

Candice!

Candice stood over Eleanor's motionless body. Pap stepped out of his truck with his spotlight aimed directly aimed at Candice. She shielded her face from the blinding light with her left forearm while keeping the gun aimed at Eleanor.

"Candice, it's over. Drop the gun. Let's talk about this."

"There's nothing to talk about, Pap," she said, gritting her teeth.

"Candice, drop the gun, God Dammit!"

"Or what, Pap? I get my life back?" she laughed. "This whore already tried to take everything away from me and I will not have it. She and James were going to shut me out and leave me with nothing!"

Eleanor's eyes opened. The voices were muffled, and the lights disoriented her. She rose to her knees and tried to stand before being struck in the back of the head by Candice. She fell back to the ground, rubbing her injury.

"Enough Candice!" Pap yelled as he slammed his door shut. He took a step forward which antagonized her.

"Pap, if you come any closer, I will kill her right here and now."

"What do you want, Candice?"

"I want her to tell me why. Why couldn't she just leave my husband alone? He was a miserable man and being his wife was hell, but he was my husband. It wasn't enough that Eleanor had been with half the parish, but she had to have my husband, too? I wouldn't have cared, but getting him to leave and cut me out of the will, leaving me penniless? That was not going to happen."

"Candice, what the hell are you talking about?" Eleanor asked from ground "I haven't spoken to him in years. I want nothing to do with him and never have."

"Don't lie now." She pulled the hammer back on her revolver, pointing the barrel at Eleanor's forehead.

"Mama!" Vanessa screamed from the darkness. Candice looked in the direction of the voice. Eleanor's eyes narrowed and her pulse quickened. She rose with both hands clenched. She swung them at Eleanor, knocking the gun to the ground. As Candice tried to pick up the gun, Eleanor leapt forward and tackled her to the ground. The women clawed at each other. The rage and hatred these women had for each other reverted them to a primal state. Candice rolled over on top of Eleanor and slammed her head into the ground. Eleanor grabbed a clump of dirt and threw it into Candice's eyes. Startled, Candice lost her balance, tripping over a headstone. Eleanor rose to her feet and kicked Candice in her ribs and back. Candice let out a grunt that was more animal than human. She crawled on the ground grabbing pieces of the Earth to propel herself forward.

"Y'all done now?" Pap yelled from his truck.

Eleanor looked down at Candice as she struggled to get away from her. She scoffed as Candice crawled in the direction of Pap's lights as though he would offer salvation when she reached him. Eleanor caught her breath as she continued to watch her rival slither toward the lights of the truck. The lights turned Candice into a silhouette. Eleanor could only make out her figure as it danced in the bright background.

"ELEANOR!" Pap's voice cut through the air. It was shortly followed by a flash of light and a loud crack. A searing pain went through Eleanor's arm. She looked down to see a red streak flowing down her left arm.

Candice rose to her feet with the gun pointed at Eleanor.

"Candice, put the gun down!" Pap yelled.

She turned to face the direction of Pap's voice. Candice fired another shot, shattering one of the spotlights on the truck. Shards of glass struck Pap's face and right ear. Michael and Vanessa emerged from behind the truck and attended to him.

Eleanor ran toward the woods. Candice, attempting to stop her flight, fired another shot, hitting a tree. Eleanor's pace quickened as she fled. She looked around and tried to familiarize herself with the terrain trying to recognize anything that could alert her to her location. The moonlight displayed nothing in front of her but trees. She had to keep moving forward. In the distance, she saw a red light.

The woods opened to train tracks, but the opposite end offered nothing other than more trees. Eleanor could not go further. She heard the snapping of branches behind her. Eleanor crossed the tracks and lay her body on the hillside, hoping should could remain out of sight for Candice. Her energy was drained. The loss of blood made her light-headed. She was running on adrenaline. She refused to die. She refused to shrink down and become a victim. She heard the footsteps approach. Eleanor heard the heavy breathing of her pursuer.

Eleanor envisioned all the possible outcomes and focused on anything that brought her back to Vanessa. The gravel by the railroad ties crunched under the feet of Candice. Eleanor lifted her head enough to see the Candice struggle to find her in the darkness. Eleanor grabbed a rock and threw it in the distance behind Candice. Hearing the rustle, Candice turned and fired another shot in the direction of the sound. Eleanor threw another rock into a different section of brush, garnering Candice's attention once again. Another shot was fired.

Eleanor rose to her feet and cautiously crept toward Candice. As she took a step forward, gravel slid beneath her. Candice turned to face Eleanor, lowering the gun on her. Candice's crimson smile returned. Eleanor closed her eyes.

Click

Eleanor's eyes opened as she realized that the gun was no longer a threat. She launched herself forward, forcing Candice the drop the gun once again. With Eleanor on top, Candice became the recipient to repeated blows to the face. Her head banged against the railroad track. Eleanor screamed, letting all her rage and fury out. The hatred she held for the Boones was finally being released. Decades of restraint disappeared. Lights flashed in the corner of her eyes. She heard the ringing of a bell and a low horn blowing. Candice's face was bloody, swollen, and bruised. Through the noise, Eleanor heard a singular voice.

"MAMA?!?!?!" Vanessa called out.

"Over here!" she called out, weakly and short of breath.

Vanessa emerged from the woods with Michael in tow. Sheriff Pap followed, holding a bloody cloth up to the right side of his face.

Eleanor stood to greet her daughter.

"Mama, are you ok?" she asked, giving attention to her arm.

"I'm fine. I'm fine. Just a little winded." She let out a deep sigh. "I could use a fucking drink."

Candice remained prone on the tracks. Pap stood across from her. He reached down to help her to her feet. As she stood, she saw the light approaching.

"Let's get you out of here."

"I'm sorry Pap, but I can't."

"Can't what? Walk?"

"No. I can't go with you."

"Candice. Let's go. I'd prefer having this conversation off these tracks and without a train bearing down on me. Come on." He grabbed her arm.

"I'm going to answer for my sins, but not to you or any judge."

She broke from his grip and, with all her strength, pushed him off the tracks. Pap tumbled backwards landing at the feet of Eleanor, Vanessa, and Michael.

Candice stood firmly on the tracks and stared down the approaching light. The horn blew louder. The brakes hissed. And the wheels screamed and sparked as the engineer tried to halt the advance of the train.

Michael, Pap, Vanessa, and Eleanor all watched as Candice's body was crushed and her life was extinguished by the train. The engineer exited the train completely panicked.

"Y'all meet me back at the truck. I'll take care of this."

The Weight of a Lie

The three sat in silence on the tailgate of Pap's truck. Michael and Vanessa used the contents of the truck's first aid kit to tend to Eleanor's wounds while they waited for Pap to return.

"Thank you." Eleanor said to Michael as she admired the bandage on her arm. Michael smiled, not knowing what to say. He was still trying to process the evening's events.

"Mama, what did she want with you?"

"I'm not sure. We've never gotten along, and I've never been a fan of her husband. Their lawyer called me earlier today to go over his will."

"Why. Are y'all related?"

"No," she sighed.

Pap approached the truck, catching part of the discussion.

"Eleanor, I think now's the time to tell her."

"Tell me what?" Vanessa's brow furled. "Mama?"

Tears welled up in Eleanor's eyes.

"Mama, what is it?"

"Vanessa, baby, we've been living a lie."

"What do you mean?"

Eleanor let out a deep breath. "I'm your mama, just not your mother. Your real mother died just after you were born."

Vanessa's face grew more confused and unsettled.

"It's true, honey. I was there that night. It was one of the first serious calls I ever had as Sheriff. There were some kids drinking at the church and someone fired a gun. Your mother was inside the church when the bullet struck her."

"It's all bullshit. The lie always was that it was just some drunk kids hanging out. The truth is that it was Candice Boone who pulled the trigger. She was always jealous of anyone who got near James. She showed up with a gun to threaten or embarrass him. She shot at him and the bullet ended up killing your mother. James asked my brother Terry to take the fall. He had been passing for white, so they all thought he was one of them and would just get a slap on the wrists. James gave

Terry some money that Father Charles gave to me before he went to jail. Your mother and I had been friends for years and your grandmother asked me to take care of you and raise you as my own. I had no family other than my brother so no one would have given a second thought to me having a baby, well, that combined with all the rumors about me. Your grandmother did not want you anywhere near the Boones. Having worked for their family, she knew nothing good would come from it. My brother was in jail for almost six months before he was murdered."

Vanessa's face turned white. Her mouth was agape. She wasn't sure what to think. Her world and everything she thought she knew about herself and those around her had come crashing down around her.

"Your mother's name was Cordelia LaFleur. She confided in Father Charles at St. Richard's church for months leading up to your birth. He met with me and would visit you often to make sure that you were taken care of. As a result, rumors started about him being the father of 'my child,' but he allowed people to talk. He knew that keeping you safe was more important than his reputation. The Church ended up relocating him in order to save face. Now that the

James is dead, what's the use in protecting the lie?"

"Pap, is this true?"

"Every word."

"Your grandmother visited you several times before she passed and remarked how much you reminded her of your mother. She said you were her spitting image in every way, even the heart shaped birthmark you have on your shoulder. It's as if she left a piece of herself on you," she said with a tear rolling down her cheek.

"Let's get y'all home," Pap offered.

Eleanor and Vanessa rode in the backseat of the truck while Pap drove them to the hospital. After dropping them off, he returned to his office with Michael. He sat down putting his feet on the desk.

"Still think this is Mayberry?" Pap gruffly asked.

"Not in the least."

"Have a seat. I have a few unpleasant phone calls to make. I need to reach Dr. Benavides to pick up what remains of Candice's body by the tracks, Sterling Doucette about her passing, and the local paper."

"What happened with that train conductor?" Michael asked as Pap sat further back in his seat.

"I told him that it was a suicide and that he shouldn't fault himself. I witnessed it and I would record it as such."

"So that's it?"

"For Candice Boone it is. She said herself that she was going to answer for her sins. That train was the judge, jury, and executioner."

Sheriff Pap began dialing the numbers for his first recipient of the evening's news while Michael turned on the coffee maker. Michael listened while Pap recalled the night's events to each person he reached that evening. Michael listened intently as Pap wove a story about how Candice Boone, distraught over her husband's death walked onto the tracks and into the path of an incoming train.

"This is how a lie is born," Michael said to himself. "A sprinkle truth spread by someone in authority to be consumed by countless others."

Michael poured the Sheriff a cup of coffee and marveled at his ability to spin the truth in order to protect the town from itself.

Clarity

Dawn broke over Laveau. The town was beginning to come to terms with the events of the past weekend. Normalcy was only slightly interrupted. Pap drove Michael to pick up his car and led him to the Magnolia to say his farewell. They were met at the front door by Vanessa and Eleanor, whose arm, although in a sling, did not diminish her glow.

They exchanged pleasantries and said their goodbyes. Eleanor assured Michael that he was welcome to come back whenever he wished with the sole condition that he stay out of trouble. He nodded and smiled before returning to his car. Pap met him, shaking his hand.

"Are you sure you don't want to hang around a little longer? Without you, it's probably going to get pretty boring around here. The most excitement I usually get is running against my deputy for Sheriff."

"Thank you, but I have to get back to work. More importantly, I need to get home so I can get a change of clothes."

"Have a safe trip."

"Thanks," he said as he sat down and buckled his seatbelt.

Michael drove off and watched the Magnolia disappear in the rearview mirror. He couldn't imagine when he first set out that his weekend would have been so filled with excitement.

Arriving home, he continued to reflect on everything he experienced and bore witness to. He opened the door to his apartment and tossed the keys on the counter. He felt worn. He sensed the dirt and sweat weighing him down. Michael walked into his bathroom to wash all the grit and grime off himself. He threw each article of clothing onto the floor. Michael stood in front of the mirror measuring his image for the first time in days. He looked haggard, grungy, and in need of sleep. The more he looked at himself in the mirror, the more he reflected. He continued to stare only stopping to look at the reflection of a small, heart-shaped birthmark on his shoulder.

He watched the reflection of his lips move as the words "Eventually, the truth comes to light," exited his mouth.

ABOUT THE AUTHOR

Donald R. Guillory is an author, historian, educator and cohost of the podcast, TheNecronomi.com. Donald is the author of *The Token Black Guide: Navigations Through Race in America*. He currently lives in Mississippi and can be reached via his website- www.DonaldRGuillory.com or via Twitter - @donguillory

Made in USA - Crawfordsville, IN
58936_9780997628111
10.12.2021 1523